CAPPING COURAGE

by Judy Wright Brooks

Best regards!

Judy W. Brooks

DORRANCE
PUBLISHING CO
EST. 1920
PITTSBURGH, PENNSYLVANIA 15238

Dorrance Publishing Co
585 Alpha Drive
Pittsburgh, PA 15238
Visit our website at *www.dorrancebookstore.com*

ISBN: 979-8-8860-4031-9
eISBN: 979-8-8860-4934-3

To Matthew, my long and trusted friend,
for his generous support that made this story possible.

INTRODUCTION

CAPPING COURAGE

Growing up in the far North in the 1930s and 1940s certainly placed a special identity on anyone. An Inuit native was required to learn skills to preserve life and benefit the family and community. Bravery and perseverance were an obligation. To the natives, Alaska, or "Alashka" to them, meant "The Great Land." That great land signified living in bitter cold most of the year, struggling against bone-chilling wind storms, starvation, and wild beasts. But it could certainly change a boy into a man.

Laura, an Inuit native, born in 1908, grew up in the frigid Alaskan wilderness. She was well acquainted with hard work and sacrifice. Her father, an Inuit dogsled mail carrier taught her the trade as she traveled with him on his routes.

I was just a young girl the first time Laura came to visit. Dressed in her beautiful handmade parka of black bear hide with white fox trim around the hood and sleeves; beaded designs in rainbow colors added the final touch. Around her neck hung a large gold nugget and smaller ones dangled from her ears. These were treasures from her grandfather found during the Nome gold rush in 1910.

Laura's generosity knew no bounds for she brought gifts for the family. I waited anxiously for the best gift of all… stories from her childhood, which riveted me to my chair wishing they'd never end.

The inspiration for this Alaskan mystery/adventure, *Capping Courage*, is owed to Laura who, through her stories, inspired in me an appreciation for this Arctic wilderness and its people.

– Judy Wright Brooks.

GLOSSARY OF
INTUIT TERMS

akutuq – eskimo ice cream

igloo – a domed winter house made from snow and ice

Inuit – northern Alaskan Eskimos

kamiks – waterproof boots made from seal skin

kupliq – lamps made from soapstone used for light and heat

mikigaq – fermented whale meat

muktuk – whale meat

nanook – native name for polar bear

parka or parkee – a hooded coat made from fur and animal skins

permafrost – a layer of ground frozen year-round

ptarmigan – grouse of the northern region

scrimshaw – carvings made by natives on ivory or bone from whales or walrus

shaman – Eskimo medicine man who practiced magic

sled dog mail delivery – all mail was delivered using dog teams and sled in the Alaskan territories until this mode of delivery ended in 1963

state trooper – law enforcement for the Alaskan territory beginning in 1941

tuktuk – north American reindeer or caribou

tundra – area of low-growing plants

tupiq – a traditional skin tent

umiak – a large, open, skin-covered boat

ulu – a traditional woman's knife

CHAPTER 1

RESCUE TO FRIENDSHIP

"Mush, you huskies!" Kort demands. "We've a deadline to meet." Stinging wind whips across a partly covered face surrounded by a fox-lined hood of the parka belonging to his father and made by Mother. Kort hasn't quite grown into it, but nonetheless, it comforts him.

Tomorrow will be the fourth and final day of the monthly Nome mail run. Soon he'll meet with Uncle Melvin for the annual spring whale hunt. Kort recalls the excitement of this hunt with Father and Melvin, but this time, Father won't be with them. Mother encourages him to go for she and sister, Nimette, need muktuk to dry for food and blubber for fuel and grease.

Thoughts cloud Kort's mind as he speeds over the frigid region; reflections of a whale hunt without Father for the first time and the fear of traveling alone. Mother can't know of this fear or anyone in the village of Candle, for that matter. How could he, a mere boy, measure up to the reputation of a man like Father? Yet here he is after the shocking incident involving his father last year. Now he must provide for Mother and Nimette, taking over Father's dogsled mail route, traveling the frozen tundra.

Kort was seventeen when assuming the responsibility of provider for the family in November, nearly five months previously. His father, Brower Olanna, had taught him the mail delivery trade believing they would continue to do this together. Now Kort is on his own. Uncle Melvin, a good friend of Brower and Mother's brother, takes the boy whaling twice a year. As far as postal delivery, no one is more trusted to carry the mail than he, for Father had been training him since age fifteen. Dogsled mail delivery has been in the family for a hundred years.

Noticing Lucia, lead dog, beginning to slow the team, Kort jumps from his place and grabs the harness to halt her. "Poor girl," he says, lifting her paws. Her moose-hide front paw moccasins, worn as a protection against jagged pieces of tundra ice, are gone. As he swabs the blood and carefully wraps them in cloth dressings from the pack, his heart fills with regret for he knows this never would have happened with Father in charge.

"Come, Lucia, up on the sled. Ride on the mail sacks to give your paws a rest." Lucia obeys with a whimper, nestling her head against Kort's leg. He's surprised to see Father's valued lead dog finally beginning to accept him as master or, he wonders, if perhaps she feels sorry for him and lacks confidence in his direction. Harnessing Sakari, second lead dog, in front, they continue on their way.

Lucia rests her anxious eyes on Kort as she lays atop the mailbags. Once in a while she gives a slight moan. "I'm sure you miss your master," Kort says aloud. He notices the deep sorrow in her eyes and her agony of losing a dog's best friend. Kort struggles with the same sadness but weeping at times seems to help. If only Lucia could talk, for she knows what happened on that fateful day... only she knows.

Kort's father had been a powerful man—both physically and in character. He had worked hard to provide for family and never complained. "Yes, Lucia, I miss him too," Kort says. "I can never hope to be as brave as he. Tomorrow we'll pass the cross Father LeRoux erected where it happened." Talking to Lucia of Father's death is easy. He's sure she understands.

Kort is looking forward to Father Joseph LeRoux's visit to the community. The Black Robe, a missionary priest from Portugal, grew up in France and was a shepherd boy from age seven to twelve. At the death of his mother, his father moved the family to Portugal where they lived with grandparents. Joseph attended a Catholic monastery school in Lisbon graduating after his senior year. As he advanced in age, he learned carpentry, self-survival, along with some medical care for the aging. Joseph's skills in caring for animals remained with him from his time as a shepherd boy. As a Black Robe he was strong and accomplished. He entered the seminary when thirty years old. After seven years he was ordained and assigned to Fatima, Portugal the first year; then on to the northern territories where he remains today. Father LeRoux's thin, lanky build offsets his brown piercing eyes, black hair brushed with gray streaks, and olive skin.

Brower Olanna and the Black Robe became respected and revered friends when Brower rescued him from a downed plane in the Arctic when Kort was twelve, and soon after Brower Olanna was baptized Brower Joseph Olanna. The pilot was bringing Brower a female Alaskan Malamute puppy, a gift from a breeder in the Canadian Yukon territory. It was widely known how much Brower prized purebred malamutes for he didn't allow inbreeding of dogs.

There was no way of knowing the exact place of the crash. However, Brower did know it was east of Kotzebue and west of the Yukon River in the Arctic. He figured it would take three days or more to reach.

There were probably injuries and, hopefully, no deaths. One wire came over the telegraph in Candle—PLANE DOWN STOP EAST OF KOTZEBUE STOP—Only Brower had the team trusted to provide rescue at this distance.

Kort remembers the conversation between Mother and Father as he prepared for the journey. "Most likely there'll be injuries. Did the pilot, Samuel Hoebel, survive? What about the precious cargo the pilot was bringing Brower? Brower had no idea a Black Robe was on board. Were they able to start a fire to stave off wolves?" Yes, it was essential to reach the crash as soon as possible.

Brower hooked the team to the sled; loaded the gear, food, and supplies. Giving his farewells to the family, he whistled to the team. "Mush, Chinook," called Brower. "Let's head to Kotzebue."

The village of Kotzebue, located in the Arctic, was the first stop. There, Brower would get a few more supplies and find out if any news had reached that area. He was sure to find a -50°F temperature once he entered the desolate north.

His walrus skin, caribou hide parka with the hood of fox fur would shield him from the bitter cold. Seal-skin gloves and boots lined in caribou hide offered warmth in this freezing region.

Night came quickly that first day for it was winter. Daylight was short. Total daylight in winter averages around five hours. In the far North the sun is absent for sixty-seven days come winter. But the midnight sun is enjoyed over eighty days in the summer.

Brower encouraged the dogs to keep moving, realizing he must stop and rest them soon. However, traveling well into the night, Chinook finally gave a long-exhausted howl. It was time to call it a day. Brower pitched the tupiq, a seal-skin tent, near a steep mass of snow. "Burrow down in the drifts, my faithful team, and rest well." Patting Chinook on the head Brower bade the dog, "Wake me early." Their rest would be short, for time was critical. He slid into his small tent, wrapping up in a bear hide.

Being startled by Chinook's determined bark brought Brower out of a sound sleep and ready to continue the trek to Kotzebue.

A few inches of new snow covered the landscape and the persistent wind proved to be a severe challenge when faced into it.

Past midday, the village of Kotzebue was visible in the distance. Chinook in the lead, turned her head to glance at Brower riding on the sled runners as if to say, "We'll make it, Master—we're almost there."

"Good boy, Chinook. You're doing fine." His praise of his lead dog always provided the best from him, Brower was certain.

Kort's father was a dependable caregiver not only for his dog team but indispensable for the family. Owning a brawny build with a five-foot-five height was contrasted by a strong character and courageous perseverance.

It was late afternoon when they arrived in the village of Kotzebue. Chinook sensed it beforehand and picked up speed in advance. Alaskan Malamutes are thought of as the true native sled dogs of the North. They are generally twenty-three to twenty-six inches in height and seventy to ninety pounds. Considered guardians of the encampments, from guard dogs to sled dogs, they are absolutely necessary to the Inuit people.

Brower drove the team to the Trading Post where he met Martin Seetook, an elder of the Kotzebue community. "Howdy," Martin said. "On your way to the crash? Word travels fast—by mouth." He chuckled.

"Heard any news by telegraph?" asked Brower.

"We can head over to the postal service and check," Martin said. "What a great-looking lead dog you have." He put his hand out to pet Chinook, but Chinook's growl stopped him.

"He's not real friendly with strangers," Brower warned.

"Let's go over to the mail drop to see if any news has come over the wire," Martin invited, tucking his hands into his parka.

"No," said the postmaster. "We've had no wire about a downed plane... just word of mouth."

"Well, I'd best head out," said Brower. "First, I'll feed and water my team." Martin waited as Brower took care of the dogs.

"Let's head to the Trading Post and get extra supplies you might use." There at the Trading Post they gave him an extra-large rope, sinew thread, needles made from bone, and wrapping gauze, arranging everything on his sled, Brower said his goodbyes and thank-yous, as he headed out of the village.

The chilling wind and recent fresh snow caused heavy drifting. Wandering from the appointed path Brower chose, could be dangerous and sacrifice precious time.

Along about early evening the second day, the wind became a gale blasting layers of snow that felt like sheets of ice. Visibility became impossible... they had to stop.

Freeing the dogs from their harnesses they immediately tunneled into the snow for protection. Brower managed to erect the tupiq and climbed in. He dozed off but suddenly woke to a soothing quiet and calm. Peering out from the slit in his tent he could see the team standing in front staring at him. They were ready to continue the expedition.

With the pleasant change of weather, they could make better time. Yes, it was extremely cold but easier travel without the wind and blowing snow.

It was midafternoon on the third day. They must be getting close to the crash if it was south of the Brooks Range and west of the Yukon River. He must stop and feed the dogs and have a few minutes rest. The solemn quiet and peace of this wilderness could take one's breath away, thought Brower. "What was that?" he said, aloud. Listening, he caught the sound of a voice in the distance... someone singing. Why, it seemed to be a chant sung in church services he'd heard before. "Come, Chinook, let's follow the sound." They headed up over a ridge a little north of their direction. Upon reaching the top, and several yards below was the plane.

Such a relief swelled Brower's heart as he spotted someone waving his arm back and forth from the wreckage. Reaching the crash, he couldn't believe how anyone could have survived.

Hovering near a fire was a Black Robe, not the pilot, clutching a wounded malamute puppy in his arms partially hidden in his walrus skin parka.

The Black Robe had splinted the pup's broken leg with long thin bone needles he found in the pilot's pack and wrapped the splint with cloth torn from his white shirt worn under his cassock.

"The pilot is dead," said the priest. "I wrapped him in an oil-skin found on board. I'm Father Joseph LeRoux and was sent to establish a mission in these parts." The Black Robe's speech was interspersed with heavy coughing but his comforting hold on the pup didn't cease.

He had found matches on the plane and supplied the fire with small wooden pieces found on board. The pilot had a supply of dried caribou and snow was melted for drinking water.

The Black Robe gave thanks to God upon Brower's arrival and they sat by the fire eating a few dried berries and dried caribou.

It was easy to tell the priest was ill. They must leave for Kotzebue in the morning. Hopefully there'd be a doctor in the village.

Brower erected the tupiq close to the plane and coaxed the priest to use it. "Here's a bear skin to wrap yourself," said Brower. The Black Robe didn't argue. He didn't let go of the pup either. Brower found refuge inside the portion of the plane still intact. He wrapped up in a couple caribou hides he found under a caved seat. The dogs had already burrowed in a snowdrift close by.

What a strange set of circumstances, thought Brower, before he drifted off to sleep. The recent events raced through his mind. He wasn't a baptized Christian, but he truly believed a higher power played a part in this. He desired to know this Black Robe better.

Brower woke to the yapping of the pup and realized it was time to head to Kotzebue. They fed themselves and the dogs—tearing up small pieces of dried caribou for the pup. The pilot's body would wait for transport. They placed it inside the plane, covering it with part of the wreckage protecting it from hungry wolves. The Black Robe rode on the sled holding the pup. Brower used his bear hide to cover them. Harnessing the dog team to the sled, Brower standing on the back runners, gave a shrill whistle and "Mush" to Chinook. The rescue was complete. They headed back to Kotzebue. The Black Robe's sleep was interrupted by coughing, but the pup wasn't disturbed. The weather was calm and they made good time stopping occasionally for rest and food. It was evening when they reached Kotzebue. Luckily, Martin Seetook spotted them as he stood outside the Trading Post.

"Whoa!" he hollered, running out in front of the team. "It's great to see you made it. Where's the pilot?"

Brower related the story asking if anyone in Kotzebue had a team to go pick up the pilot's body.

"There's a relative of his living about a mile north of here, I guess. I'll see about it tomorrow."

"Is there a doctor to look at the Black Robe? He's ill."

"There'll be the regular doc making his monthly rounds in a couple days, maybe sooner. There's the community shaman. We could get him tomorrow.

Father LeRoux perked up saying, "We can wait for the doctor, thank you."

Since the Black Robe wanted to see the medical doctor instead of the shaman, the native medicine man, Brower's getting back to Candle would be delayed. He was anxious to get home to his family.

Martin Seetook took Father LeRoux to a boarding house where he could spend the night and have a cup of bone broth.

"Some broth would be excellent," said the Black Robe. "I'm really tired." He handed Brower the pup. "I've had enough of this malamute. I'm sure you'd agree."

"Thanks for your care of her. I'll never forget it and neither will she," Brower said with a smile. Brower went with Martin Seetook to the dog shelter where Brower fed and watered his team. He told Martin he'd sleep in the shelter with his dogs.

The next morning, Brower headed to the boarding house to check on the Black Robe. The woman who owned the establishment met him at the door saying, "The doctor arrived very early this morning and is with him. You can wait in here. Would you like a cup of coffee?"

"Yes, thank you," said Brower as he sat on a chair by a small table. The coffee was warm and very soothing. He had a second cup.

The doctor appeared shortly, introducing himself. "Dr. Jarich from Nome, here," he said, putting out his hand. "Priest has pneumonia—has a high fever. I've given him medicine he can continue to take for ten days. He should be better then and fever gone. Needs bed rest for a week—maybe more. He's a tough one, though. Seems strong as an ox. He'll come out of this just fine."

Brower explained to the doc he lived in Candle and needed to get home. "I have a mail route to attend to soon and a family waiting. I've a good sled and dog team to take him to Candle where he can rest and be taken care of."

"Well, I guess," said the doc. "Keep him warm in route. Martin Seetook said you have a pup with a broken leg I could look at."

Brower took the doc to the shelter to look at the pup. Studying the splinted leg, the doc said, "What a fine job the priest did on this leg. Remarkable, in fact. It will heal fine."

The sled was ready for departure with the Black Robe wrapped in the bear hide. "You get the pup for the return to Candle," said Brower. "You're not rid of her yet."

The priest smiled, reaching out for the pup. "Come here, little Lucia, Fatima continues to look upon us."

"Lucia?" asked Brower.

"Oh yes. Do I have a story to tell you!" the Black Robe said, smiling, as they sped toward Candle.

CHAPTER 2

LESSONS FROM A CARIBOU

Kort's muscular body stands erect on the mail sled runners as he continues the route to Nome. Lucia's barking brings Kort back from his thoughts. "Yes, girl, Father LeRoux gave you the perfect name and rightly so," says Kort. "The Fatima story was instrumental in my father's baptism along with the determination it gave his favorite lead dog."

The Black Robe had sufficiently recovered from his illness due to the good care from the Olanna family. On his monthly visits to the community, he makes it a point to call on the Olannas and Lucia, of course.

The passing of time has placed upon Kort a grave necessity to speak to Father LeRoux on his concerns involving the death of his father. He counts on the Black Robe to give him the peace he so desires.

The whale hunt with Uncle Melvin will be soon. Kort is anxious for it but sorrow fills his heart that this time Father won't be there.

Images cloud his mind as he travels to a time and place on the Bering Sea, whale hunting with Father and a few others. Father had harpooned a Bowhead whale. "Throw the second harpoon!" Father hollered to Kort. Kort's aim landed in its tail.

"Good job!" Father said. "You hit the spot that keeps him moving."

What a celebration followed in the small village of Candle upon their return. The powerfully successful whale hunter returned sharing his catch with all.

Lucia's barking alerts Kort it is time to stop for the night. "Yes, girl, we'll call it a day." Lucia gave a yip in the affirmative and they halt the sled near some snowbanks. The heavy snow ridges from a recent blizzard are perfect for setting up camp.

Kort tends to the tupiq, placing whale bone to anchor the tent in the frozen snow. Once secure, he feeds the dogs and himself dry caribou from the food pack. He fills his kupliq with seal fat placing moss on top for the wick. Striking flint stones together, he produces a flame. This lamp he places in the center of the tent to provide light and heat.

The dogs dig down into the snow ridge with their heads appearing as mounds on ice. Lucia's eyes meet Kort's as he slides through the tent flaps for the night. "Sleep well, Lucia. We have a big day ahead. Wake me early, girl, and we'll be on our way."

Kort gulps down a few dried berries before wrapping up in the heavy bear hide. Neither the hide nor the kupliq seems to quell the brisk night air.

Kort tosses and turns. Frightening dreams of his father's incident wake him suddenly. Wolves howl in the distance. Any closer, he thinks, the dogs will bark. These fearless Alaskan Malamutes will attack animals ten times their size. His hand grips Father's rifle laying by his side. He hasn't used it yet to defend himself.

Father's courage is always on his mind. It gives him strength to endure the loneliness.

One of the last times he and Father had hunted caribou was near Kotzebue Sound, the summer before his death. They spotted a herd of Tuktuk, or shaggy North American reindeer, also known as caribou. They grazed on the moss-covered tundra floor and milled slowly under a forest of swaying antlers. This was the first time Kort had seen such a large herd. Along the outer edge of the herd hastened small packs of gray wolves.

"Will they attack the herd?" Kort remembers asking Father.

"No, they'll wait until a single caribou strays away, then there'll be a massacre." No sooner had Father said this, it happened. The wolves chased the lone animal ripping it apart with their teeth.

"There could be a two-fold lesson to learn from this," Father said. "It seems if we stay within safe boundaries, we don't risk being swallowed up by outside elements. On the other hand, sometimes circumstances allow us to step outside that safety circle to grow in character."

Kort's body shakes wondering what circumstances have aroused the tragic death of his father?

Morning comes and Kort is warned by Lucia's barking. It is time to get started on the last leg of their journey.

The perpetual night of the winter season has begun to give way to a sliver of light as spring shows its face. As Kort travels over fresh fallen snow, no human or animal tracks can be seen. Times like this fill him with desolation. He is thankful for his dog team. They are family to him. He loosens the hood of his parka and lets it fall to the back of his head. A few moments of fresh air will feel good.

Lucia's howls give caution to Kort of the approaching river. The cross Father LeRoux had erected at the place of his father's death will soon be in view.

"Oh, Lucia, if only you could tell me what happened here," said Kort as they reach the river. He slows the team nearby and gazes at the thick ice-covered surface with no spring thaw in sight. Next month it will be different.

Kort wipes away tears beginning to well up his eyes. His thoughts race back to when his father's body was prepared for burial by the community elders. They remarked to Mother how there was severe bruising around the head, shoulders, and abdomen. They were uncertain as to how these bruises occurred. When Brower's mail delivery to Nome was late, Uncle Melvin headed a search party to look for him. Close to Nome they found his camp and the dog team. Lucia was badly injured and had lost a quantity of blood. She lay atop the sled with the rest of the team on the ground beside her. They were harnessed together. Father's parka was near the tent. His food pack was gone and the mail sacks bound for Nome were nowhere to be found. Father's body was recovered from the icy river close to where Lucia lay on the sled.

The thought of Father suffering is too much for Kort to bear and, holding his face in his hands, he weeps.

Bending down to embrace Lucia, he cries in anguish saying, "Why, Lucia? How could this happen? Couldn't you have stopped this? This couldn't have been an accident as the village elders want us to believe. Did you get hurt trying to help Father?" Lucia's moans develop into howls. "Okay, girl, this is as painful for you as it is for me. We'll be on our way."

They arrive in Nome late afternoon. Uncle Melvin meets Kort at the postal station.

"The whale hunt must wait until next month, Kort," Melvin says. Melvin, a whaler by trade, owns his own umiak, a forty-foot wooden boat covered in walrus skins. He has a gruff manner for a man of medium build but portrays himself as one who possesses power and control. "My umiak needs repairs that can't wait," Melvin continues. "Your Mother must be patient 'til next month for fresh whale meat and blubber. That's the way things go."

"Maybe I'll get lucky and shoot a caribou or some ptarmigan to get us through," said Kort. "But we do need blubber."

"I suppose I can scrounge up a little seal blubber before you go," said Melvin. Go pick up your dogs and stop here before you head to Candle. I'll have the blubber ready then."

Sam Rawbone owns stalls for dog teams about a half-mile from the Trading Post. For a small fee, one can leave a team for a day or so. Sam will let Kort work it off by cleaning stalls. If Kort has fresh whale meat or blubber, he can trade some for Sam's services. He has left the dogs with Sam after taking the mail delivery to the postal station.

"Hey, boy, back so soon?" says Sam.

"We aren't going whaling," Kort replies.

"Oh, well then, no charge this time, son. Your dogs are here a short time. I'll get even with you next time."

"We aren't going whaling until next month," Kort says. "I'll have whale meat for you then."

Sam stands there grinning. His skin was about as red as the long red hair attached to his scalp. His straight, thin body could blow over with a gust of wind, Kort thinks. Sam's ancestors came from a place called Greenland.

"Say, did you ever find the gold nugget your father wore around his neck?" asks Sam while Kort prepares his dogs to leave.

Kort shakes his head. "How did you hear about that?"

"That's old news," said Sam. "You've got your team ready. We'll see you next month." And Sam walks away.

"Thanks, Sam." Kort stands for a moment wondering what brought Sam to ask about Father's gold nugget. Not many people know he had it or even wore it. Father always kept it under his clothing.

Uncle Melvin was busy working on his umiak when Kort arrives. "I'll stay a couple days to help if you like," he offers.

"No!" breaks in Nuevat Weyahok, Melvin's long-time fishing partner. "We don't need a little pip-squeak like you around to get in our way. Go home where you belong. We can manage by ourselves."

Uncle Melvin raises his arm like he was going to strike him. "What is wrong with you anyway? Have you gone mad?" Then, "You'd better head home, Kort," says Melvin, handing him the bag of blubber and some food for the trip. "We'll see you next month." And Melvin returns to the umiak.

Kort is a little sad as he hastens to the dog team to strap the blubber and food packs to the sled. How nice it would have been to stay a couple days to help with the umiak. He recalled through the few short years he'd known Nuevat, he was always a most unfriendly guy. "I wonder if Father got along with him?" says Kort aloud. *Although*, Kort thought, *Father was a fair and just man. He certainly wouldn't have allowed a wrong not to be righted when it came to dealing with people.*

The weather is mild as he heads toward Candle. "The weather must hold so we can make it home in less than three days," says Kort to his team.

They cross the river, scene of Father's death, without stopping. The ice is still solid. *Next month it will probably be melted somewhat*, Kort thought. Pretty soon they'll need to stop for the night but Kort hopes to travel a ways more before then.

It's late when Kort directs the team to some high snow ridges to make camp. After finishing with the usual chores, he bids the dogs good night and starts to climb in the tent.

The long, lonely howling of a full-grown Arctic wolf catches his attention. He hates that sound. Clutching his rifle, he listens to the second howl in thoughtful silence. Father always told him that wolves won't hurt you unless they're starving. *This wolf sounds starving to me*, thinks Kort. Wolves are afraid of a light at night. He takes his kupliq from the tent and places it outside the tent. Lucia is agitated by the howling and moves from her spot in the snowdrift to a place in front of the tent. Patting Lucia on the head, Kort slides inside the tent with rifle in hand.

Morning came quickly. Kort is surprised he actually slept. Pushing the tent flaps open he sees Lucia standing in front. "Poor girl," he says. "You probably didn't sleep at all."

The sky is a dark silver gray. There is no horizon anywhere. The size of every object in the landscape seems distorted. "Bad day, Lucia. No sun or stars to guide us. But you'll get us home, girl. I know you will."

CHAPTER 3

A LITTLE FOR THE WILD

It's good to be home. Driving the team in, Kort views the small village of Candle. It contains a total of fifteen similar dwellings, each on stilts, which protect them from sinking into the ground during spring thaws. No trees are used for the walls or roof—only animal skins and sod. A trading post is found at one end of the village and a postal station at the other. The multipurpose community building serves as a chapel and a school (when a teacher is available) as well as a place for community gatherings, ceremonies, and celebrations.

Before heading home, he drops one mailbag off at the postal station. He will remember to relate some of the news from people in Nome to those in Candle. This was something his father never forgot to do. It made him a favorite person to be around and very respected. Kort has to go over and over in his mind the news villagers want him to pass on. It is difficult for him to do this, but he does it for Father. Villagers come running when they spot Kort dropping off the mailbag. So, he passes on the news: new baby born to Block family, Al Kobe had surgery but is doing fine; whaling boat capsized; no one injured; Mrs. Kobush passed away. Kort is getting better about remembering, but most of all, it's great to see the happiness on the peoples' faces.

His team heads straight for their shelter when they reach home. Kort fills their water bucket and feeds them pieces of stale blubber scraps he has saved in a barrel. "You can have a break now and rest. Had a good run and I'm proud of you," says Kort as he strokes Lucia's back.

Starting up the ladder to the dwelling, he can see Mother standing at the door.

"It's good to see you, son," Martha Rock Olanna says, giving him a big hug. "I trust you had a safe trip?" Mother is stout, tough, and energetic. She is the pillar of the family—always caring, always dependable. Baptized before Kort was born, she took responsibility in teaching her children the faith. Mother is a valued seamstress not only for family but extends that charity on those in need. She makes and sells many clothing articles to village elders. This contribution helps to sustain the family. Considered a valuable dog trainer as well, it was through this that she and Father met. She doesn't speak of Father's death, but it's evident she misses him. Kort is sure she worries about him when he is on his mail route to Nome.

Nimette, his fourteen-year-old sister, sits on a bench beside a petite wooden table. The 12 x 15 square-foot home has benches against the walls for sitting and sleeping. In the center of the room, a small stone hearth is used for heat and cooking. Nimette is preparing a caribou hide for gloves and boots.

"Welcome home," shouts Nimette, jumping from her bench. How's my little brother?" She is nearly as tall as Kort and jokingly makes a big deal of the fact when he is home.

"Yeah, well Squirt," Kort says laughing, "you'll always be Squirt to me." He figures she earns the nickname.

Nimette is very studious and, aside from her fun nature around her brother, she works hard helping Mother with food and hide preparation. When time allows, her artistic talents are spent on decorating and carving ivory and stone.

"How have you been, Squirt?" he asks as he seats himself on a bench near the table. Nimette gives him a playful nudge and sits down to continue her work.

"I cleaned the dog stalls for you. Did you notice?" Nimette asks. "And Mother made your favorite treat."

"Before any treat you must first have this proper nourishment," adds Mother, handing him a bowl of wild herb and root broth. "Now, tell us of your journey." And Mother sits down beside him.

The hot liquid soothes his weary body. It is comforting to be back with family.

The next morning Kort prepares to hunt caribou or ptarmigan, whichever comes first.

"In a couple weeks, there'll be a celebration for the successful whale hunt of Thomas Tomuk," Mother says. "We are promised some of the whale meat and blubber. With what you brought from Melvin and Thomas's generosity, we'll be fine for a couple months."

As Kort set off for the hunt, Mother said, "Oh, by the way, Father Le Roux will be here in two weeks."

Kort waves goodbye as he heads out. *It will be good to see Father Le Roux*, thinks Kort. *It's been a while since we've had a chat. He's the only one who treats me like a man and I appreciate that.*

Kort arrives home at suppertime with four ptarmigan. Mother boils one for his supper and prepares the others to dry on racks in the smokehouse. Smoked ptarmigan is the best. Mother smokes it to perfection.

The whale-hunt celebration day finally arrives. All the villagers meet in the community building. No one is as powerful as the successful whale hunter in an Inuit community. The meat is always shared with the villagers.

The evening celebration continues with song and native dance. Old men read poetry of successful hunts. The young pound their drums keeping rhythm with their feet. Everyone looks forward to these events. It is the only time the community gets together to really enjoy each other's company.

At the close of the celebration, Thomas Tomuk rises and everyone applauds him. Thomas is a short, wiry man who rarely stands up straight. His posture makes him appear to be older than he really is. Kort thinks of him as being afraid of his own shadow, but he certainly never comes off that way. He is known for his generosity and by contrast, his cunning nature. Intrigue seems to hide him from truth, Kort thinks. It is hard to believe or trust what he says. You are his friend until you cross him, then enemies forever.

Fingering the jagged scar across his cheek, his eyes settle on Kort. "Thank you, everyone, for coming," he begins. "I'm grateful for this successful hunt and to be able to share this bounty with you. But most of all, I owe thanks to Brower Olanna for teaching me the skills to achieve a successful hunt."

Kort remembers a time when his father and Thomas were at odds over the way Thomas handled his dogs. He had two malamutes he was training for a lead position. He was cruel to his dogs and the smaller one suffered from wounds and poor nourishment. Brower stopped by to see Thomas one day and caught him taking a whip to his young pup. Brower grabbed the whip from him saying, "Why do you keep a dog you can't seem to train the proper way? Beating him is not going to get you the lead dog you desire."

"You don't have all the answers," Thomas argued. "If you think you can do a better job you take him and try, but I want him back."

"You'll get him back if I can't train him. But if I'm successful, I keep him and I'll give you the black bear hide that belonged to my father."

Thomas perked up for he had admired that hide for a long time. "Well, good luck. Take the mutt and I hope you make something of him. I do want that bear hide."

Father, of course, was successful and the pup, Sakari, became his second lead for the team. He gave up the bear hide and he and Thomas went whaling together on occasion.

As the whale-hunt festivities end, Kort spots Father Le Roux standing by the doorway. He hurries over to ask the Black Robe for a meeting after Mass tomorrow. Arrangements are made and Kort turns to leave when Thomas Tomuk takes him aside.

"Hey, son of the great whale hunter, you need to search for the gold nugget your father wore around his neck. It's closer than you think." That said, Thomas walks away.

It is a frosty Sunday morning as Kort stands outside the community hall waiting for Father Le Roux. He waves to a few passersby and tells Mother he'll be home shortly. Soon Father Le Roux appears beckoning Kort with his arm.

"How have you been?" asks the Black Robe as he and Kort stroll away from the community hall.

"Okay, I guess," Kort says, shrugging his shoulders.

"I realize you have a great responsibility, but I know you can handle it. Your father taught you well. His prayers for you will carry you through the difficulties. You can be sure of that."

"Oh, it's very difficult without him. Every time I pass the river… where… where…."

"Of course, that's to be expected," said the priest. "That part will always be difficult. Be patient. You're not a grown man yet. It takes time, experience, and above all, courage to develop the kind of character you saw in your father. Pray for a strong faith and perseverance to always do the right thing."

Kort feels better talking to Father Le Roux. The Black Robe says what he needs to hear. But what he really appreciates is that the priest talks to him like a man, not a young boy. Now Kort understands why his father valued the Black Robe's friendship.

The next morning, Kort ventures out to hunt caribou. Four of his eight-dog team pull the sled with Sakari in the lead. Up over the snow ridge and across the glazed tundra they bolt until Candle village is out of sight.

Positioning himself behind a snow ridge, he spots a small herd of caribou not too far below. Resting his arm against the bank, he aims and fires. The animal bolts and falls. Kort drives the team close to the kill, guts it, cuts the meat in quarters and begins to load it on the sled. Turning aside, he notices a few wolves approaching the ridge. Less than half the caribou lay on the ground when Kort hastens his team away.

Brower taught his son to care for the animals… domestic as well as the wild. The wolves enjoyed a good meal today… one they didn't have to work hard to get, thinks Kort. Mother praises him for the meat and for leaving a little behind. "You are wise like your father," she says.

The next day he cuts up the meat to dry in the smokehouse. Nothing is wasted. The hide will be scraped and cleaned. Mother will chew on it to produce softness and use it for gloves and boots. Tools, such as knives, harpoon heads, spears, clubs and traps, are made from the antlers. Scrimshaw carvings on antlers and ivory tusks are sold or swapped at the Trading Post.

That evening Kort works on a walrus tusk carving of his father and Lucia. This will be a gift to Mother.

Kort spends the next two weeks taking care of repairs at home. The dog shelter needs shoring up; a few areas require more support. Lucia's first litter is due in a couple weeks and he must make the birthing pen ready for this great event.

Brower Olanna had great expectations for his dogs. To achieve a litter that exceeds physical and temperamental expectations, these parents of the litter must hold the best performance qualities. The qualities Father looked for were: thick fur coat, long legs, large paws with compact pads, fluffy tail, correct body proportions, sweet disposition, and extreme desire to run and pull.

A male malamute in Nome was chosen—one Father had used before for one of his females. Kort knew it was time to start replenishing the team. They had never lost a pup yet due to Father's diligence and high standards. Now it is Kort's turn to prove he can handle the job.

One evening while inside the dwelling, blubber greasing his boots Kort could hear Nimette's shrieks bellowing up the ladder from outside.

"What's wrong?" he asks, opening the door.

"You better come quick! Lucia's pups are on the way!" Nimette blurts.

"What!" he hollers. "They aren't due for another week."

Lucia is in her birthing pen doing fine and has given birth to six pups—definitely fine malamutes.

"Wow!" Kort exclaims, falling to his knees. "You did wonderful, girl. What a proud Mother you must be."

Lucia continues to lay beside her brood being attentive to all—gently licking each.

Mother came running inside the shelter.

"What a glorious moment this is!" She gives Kort a hug saying, "How proud your father would be!"

The family takes turns for the next five days and nights checking on the litter and Lucia. The little mutts by the end of the first week become quite active and begin to show their true malamute traits, Kort thinks. "Oh, how I wish Father could see you," he said, watching them muzzling up to Lucia to nurse. "You must care for them for the next ten weeks. After that, Lucia, you can continue the mail runs."

Kort is notified through Candle postal station that mailbags to Nome will be ready to go in two weeks. Sakari, second lead, will take Lucia's place. He is relieved he'll have more time at home.

The next day a couple village elders come by to see the pups. Thomas Tomuk is one of them.

"You won't have trouble finding someone to take these pups," Thomas says. "Everyone knows Lucia's reputation and whose dog she was. In fact, I'll take them off your hands when you head out on the mail route."

"No!" said Kort. "They'll replenish my team."

Kort remembers his father saying, "Never give or sell a pup to Thomas."—and he meant it.

"Oh, come on," Thomas urges. "You know it'll be hard to handle all these pups—especially when you're on the mail run."

Mother spots Thomas's arrival and comes to the stalls.

"Thomas, I think you heard my son. We all help with the dogs so they will get the best of care at all times. Thanks for your interest, but goodbye."

He leaves with a scowl on his face not uttering another word.

Thomas irritates Kort. His father never trusted him for sure. Thomas always seems to know everything before anyone else. He is nosy.

This same week Kort is notified by Candle Postal Service that a veteran mail carrier servicing the Yukon River route has broken his foot and needs help on his next mail run. Kort is appointed since he has a few weeks before the Nome route.

Father had told him the Yukon River route is the most dangerous and by far the loneliest mail route in the North. The frigid weather alone is enough to discourage a man from doing the route. But wolves and polar bears pose a danger as well. Being a mail carrier even when conditions are ideal is tough and more often than not they face unpredictable ice conditions, deep snow and extreme temperatures. It is comforting to know he'll be with a seasoned mail carrier. Kort is sure he'll learn a lot from him. *Well, a new experience awaits*, Kort thought, *one that will truly be a challenge. I just hope I have what it takes to be a part of it.*

CHAPTER 4

SUSPICIONS MOUNT

Almost two weeks old, Lucia's pups are thriving on her milk. Kort begins shredding bits of dried caribou to introduce to their diet. Nimette helps daily, cleaning the stalls and monitoring the pups and will continue once Kort leaves to help on the Yukon route.

"Were you told the name of the mail carrier you'll be traveling with?" asked Mother as they sit to enjoy a cup of bone broth that evening.

"Yes," said Kort, "they told me he's Bronze Browning from North Eastern Canada. I didn't know he was coming, but I'm glad of it. I guess he's amazing when it comes to mapping a region."

"Why, your father knew him quite well," said Mother. "He was a very trusted friend. How will you connect with him?"

"Charley Watts who works at the Candle Postal Service needs to deliver a cargo sled to someone in Kotzebue and return with a smaller one. He'll let me ride up with him. Bronze will pick me up there."

The trip to Kotzebue was in two days. The Black Robe's visit was coming up before Kort's departure. Kort is hoping to talk to him briefly. He almost feels guilty taking up Father's time. The priest has so little of it. Besides attending the needs of the villagers, he must also address the local shaman. Although missionaries brought the faith to the Inuit people in the 1920s, some of the natives are very attached to superstitious beliefs. As baptized Christians, they tend to mix ancient beliefs with their Christianity.

They believe forces of nature are controlled by spirits… animal spirits. To them, animal spirits rule a person's everyday life. When a hunter kills an animal, he removes the skull, cleaning it out so the spirit will go elsewhere. Any villager who refuses to let go of these beliefs can create certain problems. Father Le Roux, realizing it was part of their heritage, tries to be gentle and understanding with them. He deals with them respectfully and with courtesy explaining why it is wrong. However, there are still a couple of shamans in Candle who refuse Christianity.

Saturday morning, Kort wakes early. Today he must pack for the trip to Kotzebue on Monday. He stands before the hearth fire to warm himself. A light snowfall covers the ground. The Black Robe's plane arrived safely last night.

Mother hands him a cup of warm broth and a few dry berries. "You might find it interesting that your father took the Black Robe to Kotzebue a few years back. The Browning's son was dying of tuberculosis. He was seventeen, same age as you. Bronze and his wife were both there then and Bronze had just returned from Nome seeking the antibiotic serum to counteract the disease. His dog team made it to Nome and back in record time, but the disease was so unchecked in growth and seriously spread that there was no hope of recovery. From your father's account, he was a very brave young man. The Black Robe baptized him and he passed peacefully. Bronze and his wife were so grateful. Bronze and your father became close friends. You know, I have something I'd like you to bring his wife."

Kort had chores to finish up Saturday evening. First, he tested the smoked ptarmigan Mother had in the smokehouse and nodded favorably to its taste.

He stands frozen as he nears the dog stalls. A trail of blood issues outside from within. Lucia lay with her front legs straddled around the pups as though embracing them. One is missing. Kort surveys the dog team. "Why didn't you let me know there was trouble? You, who can scare wolves away, can't put fear in a varmint? Or were we sleeping so soundly we didn't hear your barking?"

He stands staring at Lucia and the five pups. "Oh, Lucia, what happened? Lucia's whimpering turned to a long-drawn-out moan and tears flood Kort's eyes. "I'll get to the bottom of this, girl—you can be sure of that."

Kort follows the blood trail until it disappears before a partially frozen stream bed. Most tracks aren't visible because of the light snowfall, but traces of blood can be seen here and there.

After Mass and religious instruction on Sunday, Kort stands outside waiting for Father Le Roux. A few village boys wave as they pass by. He misses having close friends, but his responsibilities take most of his time. "It would be great to be a kid again," Kort says with a somewhat sad voice.

Father Le Roux tells him that God never gives you more than you can handle and everything that happens is for a reason. Kort is sure he is right, but somehow it doesn't make things easier. One thing for sure, he can't complain to Mother. It just wouldn't be right.

"Too bad about your pup," Thomas Tomuk says, approaching Kort.

Kort feels the hair standing up on the back of his neck. "How do you know?" says Kort. "I haven't told anyone."

"Well, someone knew. Word gets around, you know. Too bad. He would have made a super sled dog, I'm sure. Doesn't seem like the Olanna luck is holding out for you. But then it didn't for your father either, did it?" Thomas walks off.

"Oh, I'd like to give that guy a piece of my mind," Kort mutters angrily. It took everything he could muster to keep from telling Thomas what he thought of him. It was enough that his father didn't like or trust him. He certainly couldn't be respected either.

Kort sits on his haunches brooding over the pup. *Wait a minute*, he thinks, *how did Thomas know the pup was a male?* If Thomas felt pity for him over the missing pup, he sure couldn't sense it. If a wolverine had taken the pup, Lucia would have fought it and had wounds on her from the varmint, Kort thinks. The dogs would have a made a real ruckus.

The dog shelter was a make-shift covering with a large open side. Whatever took the pup might return tonight for another. He would bed down in the shelter with them.

Kort and Father Le Roux walked along a stream bed leading them up a snow ridge over-looking Candle.

"It's a quiet village. Problems do seem surmountable up here, don't you agree?" the priest says, appearing to think aloud. "Is there something you want to talk to me about?"

Kort begins by telling the Black Robe of the soon-to-be mail route in the Northern Territory with Bronze Browning. "I thought I'd have the mail run by myself. Don't really need him with me. I can handle it."

"Too bad he broke his foot but great for you to be able to help him," said the priest. "He's a good man. You'll learn a lot from him. Even your father felt humbled by his abilities."

"I feel guilty leaving Mother, but she agrees it will be a great opportunity for me. Then there's the pups. Don't want to leave them, but Nimette and Mother can handle them.

Kort went on to tell the Black Robe of Lucia's pups and the one that disappeared from the shelter.

"Yes, it's a good idea to stay in the shelter tonight," said Father Le Roux. "Hopefully you'll catch the varmint."

"Lastly, but most importantly, I don't believe my father's death was an accident."

"Well, what do you base this on?" the priest asks, somewhat alarmed.

"Mostly a gut feeling. I don't have any proof. But my father wouldn't' have allowed an accident to happen. He was wise, very wise. He was always prepared for the mail runs… in all kinds of weather. You know that to be true, don't you?"

"Yes, Kort, I know he was always prepared," said the priest. "But there's always the unknown situation, right?"

"Yes," Kort said. "And the unknown took his life."

"You can't point a finger unless you have proof," added the Black Robe. "Let matters be, Kort. If you start stirring up the pot from the past, you'll have the village elders to answer to."

"Shouldn't we follow our hearts, Father? My heart tells me my father didn't die accidentally."

It is silent for a moment before the Black Robe speaks again. "Then bravery and perseverance must be first and foremost in this quest. Gather information quietly. At the end of your search, assess the information and tell someone in authority, if what you've found merits it."

"Thomas Tomuk told me to search for the gold nugget my father wore around his neck. Thomas said, 'It's closer than you think.'"

"Yes, I remember the nugget he wore," said Father Le Roux. "It was usually tucked under his clothing… or he seemed to keep it there. I thought it was given to your mother after his death?"

"No, Mother doesn't know what happened to it. She thought it was lost in the river where his body was found," said Kort. "It was a priceless gift belonging to his father's father who found it during the Nome gold rush in 1910."

"Be careful in this pursuit of yours. It can be dangerous," said Father Le Roux. "Be on your guard not to speculate with your suspicions or to unjustly judge others. How would you like it if I visit your mother? If she's uneasy, I can stay an extra day. You need to keep your mind on the job at hand."

"Thank you, Father Le Roux." *Why do I get the feeling he doesn't think Father's death was an accident either?* Kort thinks.

On his way home, he walks along the frozen stream bed where he'd seen a few blood tracks. Today he is coming from the opposite direction, which makes it easier to see the ice-covered stream. The ice is clear in most places except for a large clump of snow about midstream. Brushing the snow away with his gloved hand there was the little pup. "Oh, my goodness," Kort says with a trembling voice. He gently raises the pup up holding him close to his face. A slight whimper could be heard. He is nearly frozen but alive. "I'll tuck you inside my parka and we'll hurry home, little guy."

Mother and Nimette are shocked as Kort burst through the dwelling door showing them the pup.

"I can't believe he's still alive," cries Nimette.

Mother begins rubbing his little body to increase circulation. As an Inuit native she is familiar with caring for frozen animals and people severely frostbitten. She applies a tincture of herbs and whale oil around his nostrils. Soon he is showing more life. "You'll be able to take him to Lucia soon, she'll be happy to see her pup," says Mother.

"Poor little pup," sobs Nimette. "Who would have done this to him?"

"Well, it wasn't a varmint. A varmint would've eaten him. There are no blood marks on him at all. But blood tracks led me to him."

"Perhaps something that carried the pup off was bleeding," Mother said. "I guess that would be possible."

"Yes," Kort adds, with aroused suspicion, "And Lucia bit that something or someone who was taking her pup."

"Oh my, Son, that's a bit carried away, don't you think?"

"No, I don't think so, but I will definitely find out."

"Sometimes things happen we have no control over." With that said, Mother says no more. She clears the table after they have their broth and does the dishes. Nimette sweeps the rough wooden floor.

Kort gathers his bear hide, rifle, and the pup and heads for the shelter.

Lucia whimpers as Kort lays the little pup beside her. She nuzzles and licks him. The pup begins nursing almost right away.

He strokes Lucia's plush thick coat. "Such a good dog, aren't you girl," he says. "Everything will be fine now. Your pup is back."

Nimette is standing behind Kort when he rises from stroking Lucia.

"Oh, I didn't hear you come out," he said.

"I want to talk to you," said Nimette. "Actually, I want to help you. Maybe if we work together, we can find out who took the pup."

"Yes," Kort says, "perhaps teaming up we can solve this and other things. I do need someone to help me. Just having someone to talk to will be great. Will you be able to sleep out here when I'm gone?"

"I will if Mother lets me," said Nimette. It wouldn't surprise me if Mother knows more about things than we realize. She probably wants to protect us."

Nimette sits on the shelter floor and picks up the rescued pup who has just finished a meal of warm milk from Lucia. Lucia watches her pup carefully as Nimette strokes his soft little coat.

"Oh, you are such a beautiful little critter. Someday you will be a giant among sled dogs. One who will let the whole Northern territory in on what greatness is. Can we call him Yukon, Kort? It just seems fitting?"

"Yes, it does seem fitting," agrees Kort. And you can call him your dog. He will be your first real training experience. I know you'll do just fine, Squirt."

"Oh, thank you little brother. I will not let you down." She gives Kort a hug and goes inside the dwelling.

Kort spreads the ivory bear hide on the ground, then feeds and waters his dogs. "We have a mail route to Nome in a few weeks, you huskies. Better get your rest to manage the long haul." He snuggles up in his bear hide with one hand gripping his rifle.

He is happy Nimette came to talk. He can sure use her confidence.

Rubbing his hand back and forth on the coarse fur, he thinks of how Father had gotten this bear hide. Hunting polar bear in the frozen Kotzebue Sound several years ago, he and a native friend had built an igloo for shelter.

Father explained that the building of an igloo was a "work" of art. Using a snow knife made from bone or ivory it was necessary to find frozen snow from one snowfall where air pockets or broken snow wouldn't be a hazard. The snow house, or igloo, would be nearly circular in form and built from the inside out. Each ice block for the walls consisted of large size cuttings. After this, ice blocks were used to make the walls; what remained was the floor. Loose snow was used to fill the cracks on the outside. A hole in the roof was made for smoke ventilation from the kupliq and an ice block for the door. Each level of the wall sloped so they all fit quite snuggly. Caribou hides were used on the floor. The dwelling took a short time to build and provided a comfortable place for the hunters.

At night they brought the dog team close to the igloo door to ward off or alert them if danger was present.

On the third morning, they rose to drink a cup of hot broth and ready themselves for the day's hunt. The dogs began to bark. The men heard a loud thud above their heads. Something was on top of the ice blocks. The nose of a bear slipped into the chimney hole. Father knew the bear could kill his dogs. He must go out and face Nanook himself. Grabbing his lance, he moved the ice block door aside and hastened out. His hunting partner stood beside the door opening with a lance in hand if needed. The dog team continued their agitated barking, circling Father in a protective manner. The bear, a very thin hungry-looking one, was crouched atop the blocks of ice ready to spring into the air. His huge fangs were visible when he snarled. Father provoked the bear to stand, then with one strong thrust of the lance drove it into the bear's chest. But the bear made one last attempt to attack his aggressor. He lunged forward knocking Father down but driving the lance swiftly through his own heart. Father's partner drove his lance into the bear's back.

"Once again Father had a great story to tell. This one is my favorite," says Kort to himself. "It really proves his manhood." *Will I ever have such great stories to tell?* he thinks.

Kort pulls the bear hide up over his head while holding tightly to his rifle and dozes off to sleep.

The morning dawns with Nimette standing over him. "Mother has hot broth and berries ready for you," she says. And yes, I can stay in the shelter at night while you're gone as long as you leave your rifle with me."

CHAPTER 5

DON'T ASK QUESTIONS

Rising from the bear hide, Kort sizes up the surrounding area. His dogs stood staring at him except for Lucia who was nursing her pups. Little Yukon was getting his share. Lucia gave a yelp to let Kort know the night passed uneventfully.

Today is the day for the trip to Kotzebue with Charley Watts. He hurries inside for a little breakfast before leaving.

"You won't leave for Kotzebue until tomorrow," Mother says, handing Kort some dried caribou and broth. "Charley Watt's left a message with an elder concerning the change. He wants you at the postal station early tomorrow morning."

"Well, I hope Bronze Browning gets the message," Kort said with concern.

"Oh yes," said Mother, "Charley will see to that. I have some caribou-hide gloves for Howard Yekut you can deliver this morning, please."

Howard Yekut is a village elder who lives on the other side of Candle. A pleasant fellow experienced in a variety of tasks. Kort arrives as Howard is scrimshawing on a walrus tusk.

"How've you been, boy?" Howard asks, trying the gloves on for size. "Just right, just right," he said, not waiting for Kort's reply. "Tell your ma she did a fine job. Sit down, boy, sit down and we'll chat a while." Howard was about as wide as he was tall and never without his bearskin hat atop his head. Howard claims he's had it for forty years. Probably so, for the black hair is falling off in chunks.

"I'm leaving for a mail route in the Yukon Territory tomorrow. Helping a veteran mail carrier who broke his foot. Bronze Browning's his name," Kort says when finding a chance to speak.

"Oh, I've heard of him," says Howard. "Has quite the reputation. What about the Nome run?"

"That will be in a few weeks," Kort says..

"You want to be careful of the ice break-up. It started in a few places already, I know," said Howard. "Nothing to mess with… remember your father's mishap."

"My father wouldn't have taken any chances. No one knew the river like my father."

"Well, Weyahok said…. Now, that's enough of dragging up the past. Let bygones be by-gones."

"Wait, Howard. What about Weyahok? Who is he? What did he say?"

"It's not important. Tell your ma 'thanks' and I'll pay her for this kindness."

Kort left Howard's with a heavy heart. It's going to be difficult learning anything from the village elders. They talk amongst themselves, but that's as far as it goes. Some of the villagers said that Father acted cowardly by allowing this accident through carelessness. Kort knew better. He must do whatever he can to save Father's honor. This he is determined to do.

Passing through the village on his way home, he spots Bill Keok mending a fishing net in front of his small make-shift dwelling.

"Hey, Kort, young fella, you come by just in time. I need someone to help me spread this net," Bill said.

"Sure," said Kort, grabbing one end of the large net, spreading it out to check for holes.

Bill uses his mending shuttle or needle carved from wood to bring the broken or shredded pieces back together.

Old Bill, as the villagers called him, is just that, old. A crop of braided white hair falls down his back. No teeth are visible and, at times, it is difficult to understand what he says. Kort thought he must have been the first Inuit in the village of Candle. Bill was the dogsled mail carrier before Brower Olanna.

"How's the fishing, Bill?" Kort asked.

"Poor, poor," said Old Bill. "Once my net is mended, I'll try again. When do you leave for Nome? Must be tough for such a youngster."

Ignoring the question, Kort decided to ask him if he knew someone named Weyahok.

Old Bill stares and finally says, "Why do you ask?"

"I recently heard his name brought up and just wanted to find out who he is. Does he live in Candle?"

With a serious look on his face, Old Bill said, "Weyahok lives in Nome. He's a guy you don't want to mess with. Thanks for your help, Kort. You'd best be on your way."

"These elders know something," Kort said aloud on his way home. "I'm sure of that."

He reaches home just in time. An early spring storm is moving in. Dark clouds shroud the sky. The wind howls blowing in sheets of icy snow. He runs to the shelter to check on the dogs, Yukon is snuggling under Lucia's jaw as one leg lays over her pup. The other pups are nestling together near Lucia's stomach. *What a sight you are*, thought Kort.

"This storm looks to drop lots of snow," Mother said as Kort came inside. The smell of rancid grease fills the air. Nimette lay on her bench bed moaning.

"What's wrong with Nimette?" Kort asks

"Her stomach is upset. Has been all day," Mother says. "I think it's a tooth."

Mother is trying to give her some blubber oil with an herb, but she tosses her head back and forth, holding her hand to one side of her face.

"Nimette, why do you hold your face?" asked Kort.

"It hurts... it hurts," Nimette cries.

"Open your mouth... let me see," he coaxes her.

"Mother, where are the pinchers Father used a few years ago on my tooth?" asked Kort, spying a badly infected molar.

Mother retrieves the pinchers. It takes a while to convince Nimette it has to be done. Then she'll feel better.

Mother makes a tincture from alcohol, herbs and grease, rubbing it on the inflamed area.

"You pull it, Mother, not Kort," pleads Nimette. Without pausing, she tells her Kort will do a good job. Little did either of them know he was scared stiff. Kort knows he has to act in place of Father. And Mother must let him be man of the family. Nimette has relaxed. The tincture is working. Bracing the pinchers onto the tooth, with one quick yank, it's over.

Kort gazes at the bloody tooth held by the pinchers. "It's over, Squirt. You were very brave," he said, while Mother packs the hole with a tiny piece of blubber soaked in tincture to slow the bleeding. Nimette sits up and tries to put a smile on her face.

"Thank you, 'little brother,'" she said with a grin. "But you are the brave one."

"Thomas Tomuk sent word he has fresh seal meat," said Mother. "This will cover the pair of kamiks (seal skin boots) I made him over a year ago. Would you go pick this up at his place before supper? We can have some raw meat for supper and you'll benefit by the strength it will give you for your long trip ahead."

"Yes, strength is needed for this journey for sure." He harnesses his team and heads for Thomas Tomuk's.

As he approaches the dwelling, he can see Thomas is busy conversing with a native Kort hasn't seen before. The two men are so intent on their conversation and something the native holds in his hand, neither seems to notice Kort's arrival. Suddenly the old scraggly native bolts away. Thomas Tomuk stands glaring at Kort.

"What do you want?" Thomas asks with an irritated voice.

"Fresh seal meat. Mother said you had some for us."

Thomas mutters something to himself and walks away. He returns dragging a skin bag full of seal meat. As he throws it onto the sled, Kort notices a bandaged right hand. The dog team becomes very excited. Kort thinks it is the strong smell of the seal meat. "Hey, team... you calm down; you know better," he urges them. The lead, Sakari, seems to be irritated by something else. She snarls at Thomas.

"Get control of your dogs," Thomas hollers nervously. "Your Father was better at it than you."

The team finally settles down as Thomas begins to walk away. "I have things to do," he said.

"Do you know anyone by the name of Weyahok?" Kort is compelled to ask as he stands on the back runners of his sled.

"What's it to you?" said Thomas. "Are you looking for trouble?" He starts to climb the ladder to his dwelling but stops midway. "I know a guy who was knifed by Weyahok simply because he didn't like the way the guy looked. Stay away from him." Thomas Tomuk disappears inside.

When Kort returns home with the seal meat, Old Bill is just leaving. Kort tries to get his attention, but Old Bill whizzes away on his dogsled without giving Kort a nod. Mother is waiting for him as he comes in the door.

"Why are you doing this?" Mother asked.

"Doing what?" asked Kort.

"Stirring up the village elders by asking questions about others. What are you looking for?"

"Truth, Mother. Truth."

"Truth about what?"

"About Father's death."

"You must accept that your father's death was an accident. It's dangerous for you to think otherwise. Accept it, Son. In the best interest of the community, we must keep peace."

After eating some raw seal meat, he went to the shelter to feed and water the dogs. He kneels down to pet Lucia and picks up little Yukon. "Oh, if life could be as simple for me as it is for you," he said, rubbing him under his fuzzy head.

Nimette comes running into the shelter very excited. "I was outside when Old Bill was talking to Mother. He was upset because you are asking questions. Said you'd get into trouble doing that. Mother stood up for you and told him you were the man of the family and had every right to. But she's afraid for you, Kort."

"Well, tough for Old Bill and all the elders," said Kort. "I'll ask as many questions as I want to find the truth."

"I want the truth too," said Nimette. "But we have to be careful, don't you think? We don't know who we're dealing with. Old Bill told Mother the elders are working on it… that's what he said."

"Okay. We're working on it too." Kort told Nimette about his day and the run-in with Thomas Tomuk. "The dogs were freaking out so bad it was hard to control them. I've never seen them act this way. His bandaged hand sure caught my eye. This mysterious guy, Weyahok, is someone we need to find out about."

"Thomas must have taken the pup, but why?" asked Nimette.

"Whatever reason, it must have something to do with Father, I think," said Kort.

"Maybe we're close to solving the little Yukon mystery, don't you think?" asked Nimette.

"Yes, but keep your eyes and ears open while I'm gone. Hope you have lots to tell me when I get home," said Kort.

Wrapped up in his bear hide that night, he tried to make sense of the passing day. By asking about Weyahok, it was decided he was stirring up trouble. Was this guy connected to Father's death? Kort felt sure he was on the right track.

CHAPTER 6

ARCTIC EXPERIENCE

It is a cold, cloudy morning when Kort arrives at the Candle Postal Station to meet up with Charley Watts. Charley is harnessing his ten-dog team to the large sled loaded down with mail and gear for the trip.

"Hey, Charley," said Kort. "You need any help?"

"No, I think we've got everything on board. Just load your things on back here and there's a place for you mid-sled. If we leave now, we should make it to Kotzebue real late tonight."

Not wasting a minute more, they were on their way.

Charley is all business through and through. He's been with Candle Postal Service for many years, not so much a mail driver; mostly a mail sorter. He and Brower Olanna were good friends.

Charley breaks the silence. "Hey, boy, does this Yukon run make you nervous?"

"Not really nervous… just wondering, I guess," said Kort.

"If you're wondering about Bronze Browning you have nothing to worry about," added Charley. "He's the best there is. I'd say he's tough, so don't let him think you're weak… he'll give you a bad time." Charley chuckled a little having said that.

On the way to Kotzebue, they stop a couple times, finally arriving around midnight. They drive the team to a dog shelter, unhook the sled and bed down in a loft for the night. They sink down in some hay after wrapping up in their hides to keep off the cold night air.

It seems they no more got to sleep, than a man's thundering voice is heard below.

"Where are you guys? Time is wasting! Get your carcasses down here and let's be moving," he roars.

Kort jumps up as quick as a wink, freeing himself from his bear hide, slips on his boots, and puts on his parka. Charley wasn't moving as quickly as he, but they both descend the loft ladder at the same time.

"Meet Bronze Browning," said Charley as they stood before him.

Bronze Browning is a man of medium build, even though his voice suggests otherwise. A mass of gray unkempt wiry hair covers his head with a shaggy beard of the same color. His clothes are well worn but orderly.

"Bronze," said Charley, "this is Kort Olanna."

"Well, well, Brower's son," said Bronze, pausing to size Kort up. "Are you ready for this, Kort Olanna?"

"I'm as ready as I'll ever be," said Kort with some hesitation.

"Come on, we'll get your gear onboard and head out," continues Bronze. "Time is wasting."

Bronze Browning has a ten-dog team of Alaskan Malamutes. His sled is heavy duty and can hold four mailbags, 50 pounds each, as well as supplies, safety gear, and a passenger or two.

His broken foot is wrapped in seal skin with a bone brace of caribou. He can stand on it for short periods.

"Well, young man, we have a journey of more than 600 miles to Dawson City, Canada following the Yukon River most of the way. There are a few roadhouses we'll stay at along the way but other times we'll use a tent. You'll be the man behind the sled steering the dogs. They've done this so many times they could do it in their sleep, but you'll be in charge of making sure they're on track." Bronze sat mid-sled with his back resting against the mail sacks. "Let's get going," he said. "Tanana Village will be our first stop on our way east."

Time passes by quickly that first day with Bronze telling stories of his experiences. "I was born in Maine in 1852," he began. "As a young man, tried bronco-busting and cow-punching in Arizona before I decided to join the Klondike stampede. Like so many gold-seekers, I failed in securing a gold claim. So, in 1887, I landed a US government-issued contract to deliver mail in the Yukon territory. I was lucky no one else was looking to get the job—no one else wanted it."

"How do you like being a mail carrier?" Bronze asked Kort.

"It's okay," Kort responds.

"It must be hard not having your father with you, but I'm sure he taught you everything you'd need to know."

"Yes," Kort replies, "no one knew better than he did." Bowing his head, he finds it difficult to continue.

"Stop the team," Bronze commands. "There's an ice break-up ahead! If you keep in that direction we'll fall through. Steer the team to the left. You get to know this area pretty well when you've traveled it enough. There'll be a roadhouse at Tanana. We'll stay for the night."

Kort gave a sharp response to the reins and the dogs moved quickly to the left. *Boy, I'm glad I'm not doing this by myself*, he thinks.

There is a pot of stale coffee on the woodstove when they reach the roadhouse. It is warm and hits the spot. A couple old-timers are seated at a rickety table in the center of the room.

Bronze greets them by name. "This is Brower Olanna's son, Kort," he said, seating himself on a bench.

One of the guys whispers something to the other and they both chuckle. The older one said, "Sorry to hear about your father. He was a good man."

"So, you knew my father?" Kort asks.

"Oh, yeah, we met him when we had some dealing with a guy named Weyahok years ago." Kort couldn't believe his ears.

"Enough of this jabber," said Bronze, "we've got an early start tomorrow. Let's hit the sack."

Morning dawns in the dark as Bronze and Kort ready the team for the long day east along the Yukon River. The cup of hot coffee helps to moisten the strip of dried caribou Kort shoves in his mouth before heading out the door of the roadhouse. A pocket of dried berries Mother packed will quiet the hunger pains before the next stop.

Bronze settles in his place mid-sled and hollers, "Mush you huskies" and they continue the journey… next stop Beaver, Alaska.

The wind is picking up and Kort can feel it's sharpness against his face.

"Bronze," Kort said in a loud voice above the wind, "who is Weyahok? Do you know him?"

"Never had any dealings with him myself but know he's trouble," said Bronze. "Your father caught him harassing an old native in Nome in a rough manner and called him on it." Weyahok told him to mind his own business and used his whip to lash against Brower's dog team just missing the lead dog. Your father grabbed the whip from Weyahok cutting it in half with his knife.

"'You won't use this whip again on your dogs or anyone else's,' your father told him."

"Weyahok told Brower he'd get even with him someday. I never heard if they had another run-in after that. Your father couldn't stand for an injustice to be dealt anyone or anything."

"My father's death was an injustice. That's for sure," said Kort.

"What are you figuring?" asked Bronze.

"He didn't die accidently. I'm sure of that," said Kort. "And I aim to find the truth."

"Well, you really have a job ahead of you, then, 'cause it will be hard to find the truth in Candle or Nome."

"Do you have any ideas?" Kort decided to ask.

"You know this wind is picking up and we'll need to get to Beaver before an Arctic fog drifts in. We've got mail to drop there and then continue on to Fort Yukon before midnight. We'll get a cup of hot coffee at Beaver and some dried caribou."

Something to eat sounds real good, thought Kort.

Their stop at Beaver was quick. They fed the dogs, dropped the mail, and drank their coffee. Kort put dried caribou and berries in his pocket and they left for Fort Yukon. Icy snow was beginning to fall and the wind hadn't died down.

"You're gonna have to go before the team to break the trail, Kort. The snowshoes are between two mail sacks. Put them on and get in front," Bronze directed. You get used to having to do this up here in the Arctic. Keep to the left of the river. The snowshoes will keep you above the snow but guide the dogs by making a light trail."

Kort straps the snowshoes on. "They were my boy's," said Bronze. "The frames are ash wood soaked to moisten them and made into an oval shape. Rawhide strips of caribou are used to attach the large hide pads for your boot placement and rawhide to fasten your boot. As you can see, they are long and wide to keep you above the snow and make it easy to glide over the snow. I've had to break the trail many times," hollers Bronze as Kort leads the team ahead. "And several times with my son along. You get used to it up here. Mail delivery's a little tougher here in the Arctic."

"That's for sure," said Kort. It's hard to see the river, he thought, straining his eyes. He is grateful for his kamiks, seal skin boots lined in bear hide, made by Mother's capable and loving hands. His feet remain warm atop the snowshoes.

The thick Arctic fog is rapidly moving in, and Kort can't make out the direction of the ice-covered river.

"Watch out, Kort!" yells Bronze. "I think you're getting too close." Bronze no sooner yells this, than the dreadful sound of breaking ice fills the air and Kort finds himself up to his knees in ice water. The lead dog takes three steps back as Bronze commands the team to "check!" He throws Kort a rope and the team backs up, pulling Kort out.

"We'll need to build a fire," said Bronze, "to dry you out a bit."

Kort's feet are numb. The ice water had penetrated his boots. He remembers frostbite stories from Father. It can occur rapidly from Arctic water.

"Yeah okay, boy," said Bronze. "Let's get the team over to that snow ridge and build a fire. There's a few branches poking out of the ridge and I've a few pieces in the gear bag."

Kort feels speechless as he builds a small fire and pulls his kamiks off to warm his feet. Times like these make him miss home.

"Rub your feet to get circulation moving," orders Bronze, throwing some more sticks on the fire. Kort is digging through his bag looking for some dry wool socks Mother had made when he spots the gift Mother had for Bronze's wife.

"Mother wants your wife to have these," said Kort, handing them to Bronze.

"How very nice of her," said Bronze. "My wife will appreciate her kindness. You know, the death of your father was and is difficult for your mother and you. My son's death still grieves my wife and me. I'll never forget your father's generosity during that difficult time. He would have given us the shirt off his back. In fact, he made the coffin for our son's burial and even lined it with his own seal skins."

Kort listens attentively trying not to let the tears welling in his eyes become visible. He is remembering his own father's coffin and how the Candle community elders took part in building it.

"Let me tell you this," continues Bronze. "Not for a minute do I believe your father's death was accidental. No one was as cautious as he was when it came to mail delivery. He didn't have a careless bone in his body."

"Thank you," said Kort.

"Keep a level head in your pursuit of finding the truth, above all, don't seek revenge as your aim in solving this," said Bronze.

"Correct me," said Kort, "whenever I need it. I can do some really dumb things."

"Pay no mind to the mishap with ice breakage. It happens. The Arctic fog displaces everything. What's important is your feet. Keep rubbing them."

"We can head to Fort Yukon now," said Kort, slipping on the dry wool socks from in his bag.

"No," said Bronze, "we'll warm up a little more before taking off. I'm not bringing you home to your mother with missing toes. Just hang on. I'll tell you a story you'll want to hear."

"Several years past," Bronze begins, "your father and I were hauling supplies to Dawson City. Something I usually did by myself, but it was right after my son passed and Brower said he wanted to go with me. He was doing this between his own mail routes. I knew it was out of concern for me. He said I needed company."

"Yes, Father, was always helping others when he could," said Kort.

"Well, to continue the story… we'd arrived in Dawson City and headed to the postal station to drop off mailbags and then headed to drop supplies at the surplus building when we spotted a guy without a parka being held over a trough by a couple guys threatening to hold his head under water if he didn't come clean with what he'd taken from them. Brower headed over to see what he could do to help.

"Hey, fellas," Brower said. "What's going on here?"

"If we wanted your help we'd asked for it," said one of them holding the guy's head down in the trough.

"Wait a minute," said Brower. "What did he do?"

"We came out of the mercantile and found this guy going through our stuff on our sled," said one of them.

"Well, is anything missing?" asked Brower.

"If it is or not, this guys a fool and he'll pay us for looking," said one.

The guy whose head was held in the trough said he was sorry.

"Father could get the best out of anyone," said Kort.

"To make a long story short," continued Bronze, "the guy with his head in the trough was looking for something to eat. Your father got the two angry men to cool down and took the hungry one to the mercantile shop, got him some food and gave him the black bear parka he was wearing. Brower had an old canvas parka on the sled and he put it on."

"Your father didn't fear doing the right thing," said Bronze. "He just did it."

"I hope I can be the same someday. I need to have an iron will like him," said Kort. "I guess that will take some growing up."

"It will be more than an iron will to get you where you need to go. It will take justice and compassion. You already have a head start. You have the prayers of your father."

CHAPTER 7

AN UNEXPECTED GIFT

The stop at Fort Yukon is just in time. Kort's feet are so sore it is hard to stand on them. There happens to be a lady staying there who is an herbalist or so she says. She takes a look at Kort's feet and rubs an herbal tincture on them… really dousing the toes. Before they leave the next morning, she douses them again. She shakes her head and says Kort shouldn't be standing on them. Handing him a bottle of tincture she tells him to use it twice every day.

"We have a mail drop at Circle next. It'll be quick; then on to Eagle," said Bronze. "We'll stop for something to eat there and a cup of hot coffee," Bronze continues. "We'll get your feet doused with that herbal concoction and head to Dawson after we snooze a couple hours. We have to speed up a bit for we're a day late getting to Dawson."

"Sorry I fouled us up," said Kort.

"Hey, things happen. I've told you that," said Bronze. "Everything will be fine."

They arrive in Dawson City in the early morning hours. The town isn't awake yet so they head for the dog shelter where they can rest the team and themselves for a couple hours.

It's good to get off my feet, Kort thought as he lay down on some hay and wraps up in his bear hide.

It seems he no more closes his eyes, than Bronze is hollering to get up and go for some breakfast. Kort doesn't argue. He is starving.

Dawson City is the biggest town they've been in since they left Kotzebue. They eat a hearty meal at Beulah's Diner that morning. The food renews Kort's energy, giving him strength to continue.

They drop the mailbags off at the postal station.

"Where's Doc Kittredge?" Bronze asks the post master.

"Oh, that's not necessary," said Kort.

"Yes, it is," said Bronze.

They find the doc at the infirmary checking on some patients.

The doc removes Kort's socks as he lay on a cot. "You have a couple toes on your left foot with a little infection but they should be better in a couple days."

Kort shows him the bottle of tincture he's been using for his toes.

"Yeah, I think this is a good recipe for you," he said, smelling the remedy. "Keep using it. Make sure you keep your feet dry, young man."

After seeing the doctor, they head to the mercantile for supplies. Kort gets some horehound sweet treats for Nimette. They pick up mailbags at the postal service. As the bags are loaded on the sled, a native approaches from across the road.

"You Brower Olanna's son?" asks the native. Kort stands motionless.

"What's it to you?" asks Bronze. "Who are you?"

"Mel Scrubs," said the native, "and I met Brower Olanna a couple years ago in Nome."

"He's been gone over two years," said Kort.

"Yeah, well, it must a' been his last trip to Nome. He told me he had a son in Candle. I heard your name spoken yesterday. When I spotted you across the road, I figured you must be him."

"So, what can we do for you?" asked Bronze, sounding a bit irritated.

"I have something that belongs to Brower. I'll give it to you," said the native, slowly reaching into a deep pocket of his parka.

Kort is fascinated by the stitching on the parka which held his attention while waiting for the native. *Where have I seen that before?* he thought.

Opening his hand, the native displays a beautiful ivory knife made from a walrus tusk with a detailed black scrimshaw carving of an Inuit boy and a dog. The native hands it to Kort who holds it tenderly rubbing the smooth, shiny surface. "Your father had seen some of my carvings on one of his trips to Nome. He'd check in to see how I was doing when he came through. Your father hired me to make this. Said he'd be back in a month to get it. Said he'd bring his boy with him. But he never came. I heard what happened… very sorry."

"It's wonderful," said Kort, continuing to stroke the surface.

"You did a beautiful job," added Bronze.

"Did my father pay you for this?" Kort asked.

"Oh, yes, in many ways," the native admits. "Not only kindness but food from the mercantile in Nome. I was destitute."

Bronze, staring at him, finally recognizes who he is. "Well, I'll be! You're the man he gave the parka you're wearing, aren't you?"

"Yes," said the native. "I've never forgotten his generosity."

Kort held out his hand stroking the arm of the Black Bear parka. "My father never came back from that mail run to Nome. He wasn't wearing the parka when his body was recovered. Mother wondered what happened to it. She'll be happy to know. Thank you," said Kort. "I'll never forget you. If you're ever in Candle, come see us. Mother will be happy to meet you."

The native, smiling, walks away. Kort continues to hold the knife. "Father made this for me," he said aloud. *He didn't deserve to die*, kept rolling over and over in his mind. "Someone will pay for it I'll make sure of that," he said, aloud.

"What did you say?" asked Bronze.

"Nothing," said Kort.

"Let's get on our way, then," said Bronze.

With mailbags loaded along with all the supplies, they headed out of Dawson City on their way back home.

"We'll stay at Circle tonight and head for Beaver tomorrow," said Bronze.

Travel is a little better going back than it was coming, thought Kort. Or maybe he was just anxious to get home. At Circle they eat a good meal and get a few hours' sleep. Kort's feet are much better. The redness is almost cleared up. Bronze takes a look at them and nods his approval.

"You're luckier than I was," he told Kort. "Quite a few years back, when I was pretty new to the mail runs, I lost a few toes to frostbite. It's a good thing it was just a few. It could have been much worse. On that trip I was heading east from the Yukon-Charley Rivers when I suddenly felt my sled being pulled into a hole in the ice. I called to my dogs to climb out of the water, but by the time they scrambled free I was drenched from head to foot. I was still several miles from the next roadhouse. Within seconds my clothing was frozen solid. By the time I reached warmth and shelter my face was frostbitten and my feet badly frozen. At the roadhouse I bound my blistered and swollen feet and continued my journey to Dawson City for my mail delivery. When I arrived, I hobbled into the postal service with marked bloody footsteps. The doc in Dawson wanted to amputate my feet, but I threatened him if he did. In the end I lost four toes but I've continued my mail delivery and kept my feet."

"You're a tough man," said Kort.

"Maybe tough but, I guess, mostly proud," Bronze admits. "But I thank God every day for letting me continue my mail delivery."

Their next stop is Tanana. They drop mail and pick mail up before heading to Kotzebue. They are tired and hungry, but the thought of home almost convinces Kort to continue without any more stops. They eat and sleep at Tanana. In the morning, a cup of good strong coffee stimulates their tired bodies to finish the journey. *Can't imagine how Father was able to do this mail route for all those years*, thought Kort.

They reach Kotzebue late the next day. Bronze's wife is there to greet them. She is pretty much the way Kort imagined her. A little taller than Bronze but appears stout and strong. She has a kind but tough nature, which comes forth when she speaks.

"Well, well," she begins, "how good it is to see the both of you. I trust you had a successful journey without too many problems?"

"Oh, just the normal," said Bronze. "Here's a gift for you from Kort's mother."

Mrs. Browning holds them in her hands gazing at Kort. "You sure look like your father," she said. How grateful we are to have known him. Oh, thank your mother for these wonderful seal gloves. She must have known how much I need them and they fit just fine."

"You know young man," said Bronze. "Something tells me you need these snowshoes much more than me. I'm sure our son would think so too. Besides, I have another pair."

Mrs. Browning nods.

"Thank you," said Kort. "I've learned a lot on this trip."

The next day Charley picks him up at Kotzebue and they head back to Candle.

On the trip home, events churn over and over in Kort's mind. Would Nimette have found anything out about Yukon's disappearance, he wonders. *It was Thomas who did it, I'm sure. But why? Hatred of Father for some reason. Bronze doesn't believe father died accidently. Neither does Father Le Roux. I'll find out. I don't care what it takes. I'll find out and he'll pay.*

Mother and Nimette are waiting for him outside the stalls when he pulls in. How happy they are to see him and hear stories of the trip.

Mother went inside to prepare the evening meal. Kort goes to the dog stalls followed by Nimette. "Man, these pups have grown," he said excitedly. "You did a good job." Lucia nuzzles her head against Kort's leg as he holds little Yukon. "Yes, girl, I missed you too," he said kneeling to pet her.

"Okay," he said, "What do you have to tell me, Squirt?" Nimette has been fidgeting since they came into the stalls.

"Thomas Tomuk came by a few days after you left," Nimette begins. "I was finishing up in the stalls. He went in to see Mother. I followed him in case I needed to help her but more I wanted to know why he came. He said he wanted Yukon. Said our father owed him a dog."

Kort squats down on his haunches with utter annoyance covering his face. "How dare him even think of asking… how dare him. What did Mother say to him?" he asks, rising up.

"She told him he'd have to ask you. Then Thomas became angry. Said she shouldn't let her son make decisions he's not mature enough to make. He told her he'd take the pup now." Mother told him, 'Over my dead body. Kort is the man of this house and you will ask him.' She asked him how he injured his hand. 'None of your business,' he told her. 'Just remember, Brower owes me a dog and I plan on getting one.' He stormed out the door stopping at the stalls to look inside. Sakari began to growl and so did Lucia," continues Nimette. "Mother and I had followed him out and could see the dogs. Before he left on his sled, Mother told him he needs to show some respect to you and our household."

"I think Mother knows more than we think, don't you?" asks Nimette.

"Yes, she is very wise," adds Kort.

"So, what will we do next?" asks Nimette.

"Good job, keeping your eye out, Squirt. Keep close to Mother. If anything comes up while I'm on the Nome mail run, make sure you tell Mother. I'll see Father Le Roux before I leave. I'll tell him all about this," said Kort. "You can always talk to the Black Robe about your concerns."

That evening Kort shows them the knife the native, Mel Scrubs, made and the story behind it. Mother is happy to hear Father gave him the parka. Mother and Nimette take turns holding the knife. Kort can see tears building in Mother's eyes. Quickly he jumps up and pulls the horehound sweet treats from his pocket.

"Here's some sweets I brought you from Dawson City," he said, bringing a smile to their faces.

"Father Le Roux came by a couple days after you left… said he wants to check on us and the dogs," said Mother. "I think he misses Lucia. She brings many memories back to him. I thought it strange, though, that he mentioned someone named Weyahok. Said he'd met him with Thomas at the mercantile. Didn't you say you'd heard the name, son?"

Kort's face felt heated. He walks back and forth in their small dwelling. *I've a week before my Nome mail run*, he thought. *Day after tomorrow I'll go see Thomas.*

CHAPTER 8

DOG TAG E-4-1345

A howling wind ushers in the morning along with a few snowflakes here and there. Kort finishes his chores and tends to the dogs. He sharpens the sled runners for the Nome mail run and mends some dog harnesses.

Howard Yekut pulls up on his dogsled as Kort leaves the stalls. "Give this seal skin to your ma," he said. "She'll put it to good use. And this is for you." He places a polished amulet made from a wolverine tooth in Kort's hand. Kort stares at it not knowing what to say. Many of the natives, even though Christians, continue to delve into the superstitious practices of their ancestors. Kort's family, being instructed by Father Le Roux, knew it was wrong.

"Thanks, Howard, but as a Christian I can't take this," said Kort.

"I'm just concerned about your safety. You'll need all the help you can get. Good luck, son," he hollers, giving a yank to the harness and whizzing away.

Kort stands tossing the amulet over and over in his hand. Looking closely, he can see the carving of a bear skull on one side and the initials K.W. on the other. *Who can that be?* He wonders. There are many questions he'll have when he reaches Nome. The amulet is one of them.

A visit to Thomas Tomuk's will be tomorrow.

"Why are you going to see Thomas?" Mother asks as they eat their breakfast of dried caribou and berries.

"Just have some questions I want answers to," said Kort.

"Mind your manners," Mother urges. "Remember, he's an elder of the community."

"Yes, Mother, I know."

Kort shows Mother the amulet Howard had given him.

"Well, I guess Howard's concern for you goes beyond right or wrong," said Mother. It's important to know he means well. We must respect the traditions of our ancestors realizing not everyone understands why, as Christians, we must take care to follow truth. As for K.W., no, I don't know who that is."

Pulling into Thomas's place, it looks deserted or at least no one around. Kort parks his team and walks into the dog stalls. *This is a mess*, he thought. *Hasn't been cleaned in a while.* He can tell the dogs are hungry and thirsty. He gets them water, which they lap down quickly. Looking around, he spots a metal disc attached to a string of rawhide, which lays on an old burlap pouch near the stall entrance. He picks it up quickly putting it in his parka pocket when he sees Thomas coming.

"What are you doing here?" he yells.

"Looking for you. I have a few questions to ask you," said Kort. "And I gave your dogs some water."

"I take care of my dogs. Don't need your help," Thomas said angrily.

Thomas took his whip off the pole and begins cracking it in the air… driving Kort backwards from the stalls.

"Your father owes me a dog and I plan to get one," Thomas insists.

Kort can't hold out any longer. "Is that why you took my pup and tried to do away with him? Why did you hate my father? Who is Weyahok?" Kort yells.

Thomas drops the whip. Approaching Kort face-to-face, he said in a forceful restrained voice, "You'll drop this search if ya know what's good for you."

Kort ran to his sled. "You haven't heard the end of this, Thomas," he hollers in a choking voice and hurries away.

As he heads in the direction of home, he can see the Black Robe approaching driving a team toward him. They pulled alongside each other and Father Le Roux can see Kort is quite distressed.

"Let's go to the community hall where we can talk," said the priest.

"So what went on back there?" Father Le Roux asks as they sit down on a bench.

It felt good to talk to the Black Robe and get everything off his chest.

He tells him of the confrontation with Thomas and shows him the disc and the amulet.

"So, you took this disc from Thomas's place? Why?"

"Because my father had one and I want to show Mother to see if it was his," said Kort.

"So even though you think you have proof of something… you really don't yet. You're getting worked up and you're going to get into trouble."

"I know you don't think my father's death was an accident…."

"Wait a minute, Kort. I never told you that. You're jumping to conclusions," said the Black Robe. When you talked to me some time ago about your concerns, I told you to go quietly and slowly. You are doing neither."

"I'm tired of no one caring or trying to protect my father's honor. I'm not going to let someone get away with evil. I'm going to make sure someone pays."

"Promise me one thing," said the Black Robe. "That you confide in me when you think you have proof of something… and take heed in my advice. You are not always going to be right. Remember… humility is a virtue."

Kort nods but says nothing further. He gets on his sled and heads home.

Nimette is waiting for him as he drives the team in. "Are you all alright?" she asks. "You don't look so good. What happened?"

Kort unhooks the dogs from their harnesses. They devour the water Nimette gives them and lay down to rest.

"Answer me, please," said Nimette. "What happened?"

"Thomas threatened me," said Kort. He told her what happened and what he had said to Thomas. When I left Thomas's, I met Father Le Roux coming to find me. Mother must have told him where I was. He said I must be patient and careful about finding proof. Well, I've found proof. I know who killed our father."

"What are you going to do?" asks Nimette.

"Thomas will pay, that's what I'm going to do."

"You should listen to Father Le Roux… listen to him. Our father trusted him," said Nimette.

"I found this in Thomas's dog stalls," said Kort, taking the metal disc from his pocket. "I remember Father having something like this. That's why I took it."

"Is that a dog tag?" asks Nimette, puzzled.

"Yes, you could say that. A dog tag for the Inuit people living in Canada. That's how they were identified there. The people didn't like it. Many of them moved from Canada and settled here. Father wore it out of respect for Mother's family."

"Are you going to show Mother?" asks Nimette.

"Yes, she'll know if it's the one Father wore."

"And if it is, what will you do?"

"Then we'll get that figured out."

After their evening meal Mother and Nimette wash the dishes and sweep the floor. Mother had been very quiet and hadn't even asked Kort how his visit with Thomas went.

"I have something to show you, Mother," said Kort, taking the disc from his pocket.

"What! Where did you get this?" she said, turning it over and over in her hands. "E-4-1345… E-4-1345," she keeps repeating. She turns and walks over to her bench bed placing the metal disc on a little shelf. She turns to Kort, saying, "You stay away from Thomas Tomuk." She lays down on her bench and goes to sleep. Mother knows where the metal disc comes from.

Tomorrow is Sunday services and Kort will talk to the Black Robe afterwards. The Father needs to know the metal disc was his father's. He wants the Father to know he needs his guidance. Nimette is right. They can't do this alone.

Mother and Nimette give a wave to Kort as they head home while he waits for the Black Robe.

"Well, young man, how are you doing?" asks the priest appearing from the corner of the building. "You've never told me about your mail run with Bronze Browning."

So, they walk out of the sight of others and Kort tells the Black Robe all the good along with the difficulty of the long trip to Dawson City.

"Well, your experience with Bronze Browning should carry you a long way," said Father Le Roux. "Remember to always think if what you are doing or intend to do is what your father would want," continues the Black Robe. "Would your father be happy with your bitterness? I don't think he would."

"I know he would tell me that truth will prevail. He told me that many times," said Kort.

"You must let your mother know what you are planning to do. Make sure you do this."

"Yes, Father, I will try to do that," said Kort, "but, I am the man of the house and I have an obligation to my father."

A cold arctic wind blew in some white powder the next morning. Kort is anxious to start out for Nome even on a day like this and he can't delay the trip any longer. Spring is yet to show its good side. But then, in the far north, spring and summer sneak in and out relentlessly.

Mother lay his packed skin bag of cloth dressings, blubber oil herb salve, dried caribou and ptarmigan, and dried berries near the door. Plenty for him and the team for four days. On the return trip Uncle Melvin will supply the food. They will go whale hunting for a couple days before he heads back to Candle. Kort looks forward to that. He also plans to do some investigative work while in Nome.

Kort loads the sled with supplies, gives a hug to Mother and Nimette and harnesses the team to the sled with Sakari as lead dog.

With a hardy wave to Mother and sister, he glides past their dwelling.

"Take good care of the pups and Lucia," he shouts as he drives the team out of sight.

At the postal station, four full bags of mail, each weighing over fifty pounds, are loaded on the sled.

"Huge shipment to Nome this trip," said Charley as he helps load the sled. Charley is mindful of how Kort has matured since the Dawson trip.

"Yes, sir. It's a good thing these Alaskan Malamutes can carry heavy loads. There's always a smaller load coming back. But we'll probably be hauling whale meat as well. See you in a few weeks."

Giving a wave, Kort heads off, leaving Candle for the wilderness.

The vast Arctic landscape lay ahead as Kort drives the team on. This is always when his stomach aches and his heart feels heavy. Being alone—he and his dogs—against the broad expanse that stretches before them. On the other hand, time now to think and plan what can be done to solve the mystery of Father's death. He feels alone in this as well, except for Nimette who assures him of her support.

In the evening of the first day, he makes camp against a snow ridge. The wind has picked up and the team is tired.

"Time to feed you and settle in for the night," he said to them.

With the tupiq erected and a fire in the kuliq, the team chows down on some seal blubber and Kort satisfies his hunger with dried ptarmigan.

It has been a long day. Kort's body seems to ache with every movement. Bidding the dogs to burrow in the snow pack for the night, he settles in the tupiq. He can't think of anything but sleep.

A fiercely blowing wind and Sakari's yelps brings Kort from a sound sleep. Looking from the slit opening of the tent he can see Sakari pacing back and forth. "Sakari, burrow back in. I need a little more sleep," he tells him. Reluctantly, Sakari burrows back in the snowbank.

In the morning hours, Kort wakes hearing Sakari's barks. "I'm coming, boy, I'm coming. Be patient. He manages to crawl from the bear hide with a cold sweat and aching body. He stands up but falls back on his knees. Trying again he makes it to the tupiq passage opening to care for the dogs. Sakari was right there. He seems to sense Kort's illness.

After feeding the team, he rummages through his pack to get the flint stones and moss to make a fire. A good hot cup of moss tea and seal oil is what Mother would order. He sits in the tupiq drinking the tea, praying it will give him the needed strength to travel on this third day, but it doesn't seem to quell his shivering body. A fever and dizzy spells trouble him. He remembers the salve Mother put in his pack. Mother made it using the herbs Goldenrod, Yarrow, and Bunchberry mixing in some seal oil to make a paste. Kort rubs it on his shoulders and neck.

He hasn't ventured too far in route when standing on the sled-runners is becoming impossible. Stopping the team, he slouches slowly off the runners and drags himself to lay atop the mailbags telling Sakari, "You're in charge. I must rest my aching body." Kort never remembers feeling this sick before. Hallucinations, brought on by a high fever, make it difficult to sleep. Kort can see his father being held under the icy river by a strong-armed man. Bubbles are floating up from the river bottom as his father takes his last few breaths. Lucia keeps barking trying to break loose of her harness to save him. She is beaten back by someone. Lucia lashes out….

Kort wakes gasping for air as Sakari licks his face. The dogs formed a semicircle around him, harnesses attached. He sits up to find they have reached the river's edge.

CHAPTER 9

PAYMENT FOR CONDUCT

"You did well," said Kort to his team stroking Sakari. "You took good care of me. We'll cross the river tomorrow. Let's make camp here. I'll shoot a varmint for our meal. Some fresh meat will taste real good, right, Sakari?" His rumbling stomach tells his hunger.

There wasn't much light left in the day. Kort proceeds away from camp with rifle in hand. With each step he partially sinks in the crusted snow. Just ahead he spots something lying in the snow. Raising his rifle, he approaches cautiously. He finds a dead moose partially eaten. Wolves most likely killed it and they'll be back for the rest. He slices some meat from an untouched portion, placing it in the meat sack he'd brought along. Wolves' howls tell him he best be on his way back to camp. Running on the crusted snow is difficult with a meat sack over his shoulders. Rising from a fall, he can hear wolves getting closer. With two shots from his rifle, the wolves flee. Kort breathes a sigh of relief. That night he and his dogs dine on raw moose meat, saving enough for tomorrow.

Before turning in, Kort is entertained by the Aurora Borealis in the northern sky. A vivid display of greens, pinks, and yellows dance across the heavens. His father told him the Inuit people of long ago believed the lights were a sign of approaching doom. How could that possibly be? thought Kort. He was on a mission to save his father's honor. There could only be doom for the person who killed him.

Kort rests well that night. The fresh moose meat was the remedy he and the dogs needed. They chow down the remainder of moose in the morning and make ready the sled and dogs for departure.

It is difficult viewing the river as he stands at the edge… the river father perished in. Sakari, beside him, gives a whimper. Kort chooses a place to cross where the beginning of ice break-up isn't evident yet.

Not wanting to take any chances, Kort decides they will cross the river separately. He'll send four of the dogs with a mail sack each. He and Sakari will go last with the sled.

Kort, down on his knees, moves cautiously across the ice, pushing the sled with Sakari in front. He feels the ice rumble a little midway. He pauses a moment but everything seems stable so he moves on. What a relief he feels once they are all across. It wouldn't matter how many times they cross that river, it will never be easy. A ways from shore he feeds the dogs and eats a little himself before they head on to Nome.

Uncle Melvin is at the Nome Postal Station when Kort arrives. "Good to see you, young man," said Melvin, giving him a strong pat on the back. Melvin helps him unload the mail sacks. "How's your mother?" he adds.

"She's doing fine. Sends you her best," said Kort.

"Are you ready for the whale hunt?" asks Melvin. "We'll leave in a couple days after I tend to some business."

The anticipation of the whale hunt stirs in Kort's mind as he drives the team to Sam Rawbones where he'll stay to take care of the dogs. This will be the first time without his father, but he looks forward to getting a whale. Uncle Melvin always gets his whale on a hunt.

The next morning, Kort strolls through Nome. It is larger than Candle with a few businesses dotting the road. A trading post is at each end of the town.

Kort stops in at Kamik's Trading Post. John Kamik was a good friend of Father's.

"Hello, young fella," said John, as he sits on a stool punching holes in a leather strap with an awl.

"Haven't seen you around for a while."

"Been busy," said Kort, looking about. He can see Kamik's trading post carries more supplies than ever.

"Business must be good," said Kort, rubbing his hand across a Hudson Bay wool blanket.

"Has been a fair year," said John. "Lots of newcomers in the area. Many stay to hunt and trap."

"Say, John, do you know someone by the name of Weyahok?" asks Kort.

John stops working on the leather strap and looks at Kort. "Never had any dealings with him, but hear he's a tough character. Your Uncle Melvin's fishing partner, Nuevat, knows him. They're related."

"Say, I have something to show you," said Kort, with the amulet in hand. "You know anyone with these initials?"

"Yes, I'm sure its Konok Weyahok," said John.

Kort explains how he got the amulet and, also, his concerns about his father's death.

"Son, you're messing with fire. Let your father rest in peace."

"He can't rest in peace if he's considered a coward. His honor must be saved."

"Your father had only one enemy I know of—Konok Weyahok. Everyone knew how much your father valued his malamutes.

"That's for sure," broke in Kort.

"Bet you didn't know your father traded a malamute? Yes, a malamute for one of Weyahok's huskies. Thomas Tomuk had convinced Brower that Weyahok was a good guy. So your father, always wanting to give someone a chance, went along with the trade. He knew he'd do well training the husky and he understood the malamute would receive the deserved attention. But within a month's time, the malamute died from abuse. Konok claimed the Malamute was defective and wanted the huskie back. Brower met up with Weyahok and beat the guy up."

Kort is stunned. He'd never heard this story before. *I wonder if Mother knew,* he asks himself.

"This was a grave humiliation to Weyahok and he never got over it," John went on. "Well, the whole town knew about this by the end of the day and they both paid for it in one way or the other."

"What do you mean they paid for it?" Kort asked.

"Your father was summoned by the elders, and Weyahok… well, he lost any good to his reputation he had before then. And as for your father, he had to go before the community elders. He was told that he should have gotten permission to reprimand Weyahok. The elders said he must pay Weyahok a month's wages. Money was hard to come by, but Brower didn't complain. That was the last time I saw your father angry. It wasn't long after that he became a Christian."

Kort begins thinking of a time several years back when Father corrected him for accusing Nimette of something before the facts were known. "Don't be a bully," Father said. "Someday you'll pay for it."

"I'm glad you told me this story," Kort said to John.

"We all have our stories," said John. "You can certainly believe this one. You like stories? Go see Maude Blaufuss. She's a German lady who's lived in Nome many years. A good woman… runs a boarding house. Rents rooms on the other side of town. She knew your father."

"I remember Father speaking of her," said Kort.

"Go see her," said John.

Kort walked away thinking about his father beating someone up. It was hard for him to believe.

CHAPTER 10

STRUGGLE FOR COURAGE

Maude is using a broom to beat the dirt out of an old rug draped across a clothesline when Kort arrives. A sign in front of her place read—NO VACANCIES.

She is a short, plump lady with silver hair tied back in a knot. A faded flowery dress of sackcloth and a well-worn apron around a full rounded waist identify her as a hardworking woman.

Maude stops beating the rug when she catches sight of Kort. "May I help you, young man?"

"I'm Kort Olanna," he said.

"Oh, I know who you are… look just like your father. I'd recognize an Olanna anywhere. And I can guess why you're here. Come inside and we'll have coffee and cookies."

Maude's house isn't an ordinary one you'd find in the Northern territory. A particular peaked roof with lattice trim gives the front porch an inviting appearance.

"My husband built this house. Was his way of bringing Germany to Alaska," said Maude.

She motioned Kort to sit down while she heated a pot of morning coffee on her cookstove. The pungent odor of bear grease cookies rises from a plate placed before him. Maude's kitchen is a warm, welcoming place, he thought, as he looks at the variety of things hanging on the walls. One thing above the table catches his eye.

"I wondered if you'd notice that," said Maude. "Your father made that before he married your mother. He gave that to Mr. Blaufuss and I when we married. She took it down laying it on the table. It was a knife of carved whale bone with scrimshaw which read, To Blaufusses from Brower.

"My father loved to carve," Kort said, turning the knife over in his hands.

"Yes," Maude adds, "he was a real artist. It's very special to me. Was to my husband as well. He passed away a few years ago. Built this house as I told you and also the two trading posts in Nome.

"My family left Germany to settle in Alaska when I wasn't even born," Maude continues. "The stories of the Gold Rush in Nome excited my father. Got him thinking he could make a better living for his family. Well, it didn't work out so well. My mother's heath suffered and my father passed a year later. To make a long story short Mr. Blaufuss came from Germany to Kotzebue as a tradesman to teach the natives the art of building. That was a struggle because they naturally had their own way of doing things. Anyway, that's how we both ended up in the far north."

Kort is feeling real comfortable at Maude's. He's filled himself with cookies and drank down two cups of coffee.

"So, I suppose you're on a mission for your father?" Maude asks as she sat at the table with him. "Well, go ahead. Tell me all about it."

Kort takes a deep breath and begins. Words seem to come quite easily. It is like talking to a close friend or maybe it's the gentle way she listens. When he finishes, Maude pauses a bit, staring at him.

"You know," she begins, "I've a good story to tell you. One that perhaps will be helpful to you in the future. It's about a boy, a little younger than you, who many years ago learned courage the hard way... the way most of us have to learn. The boy, for that's what we'll call him, was not pleasing in his father's eyes. To hunt, he was afraid. The sight of blood made him cringe. He became ill when his father insisted he help cut up the day's kill. His father looked with disappointment on him as did the village elders. The boy knew to become a man, he must first become a hunter. So, one day in early spring he set out to hunt seal and return with his kill. His father allowed him to go, knowing he might never see his son again. The boy hastened to the ice field with his dog team and father's spear. The first day, he and the team were stranded on a large ice chunk, which broke away from the ice field. The second day, the food pack disappeared in the icy water."

"Boy, everything is going wrong for him," Kort breaks in.

"Well, it gets better," assures Maude. "On the third day, he speared a good-sized seal. He and the team pulled it up onto the ice chunk. But in the process lost his father's spear in the deep waters. He carved off slices of fresh meat using his mother's ulu she'd loaned him. They feasted on the seal meat filling their empty stomachs. The following morning the ice chunk had found its way back to the main. The boy, team, and seal meat arrived back in the village to a jubilant welcome."

"That's a great story, Mrs. Blaufuss, but what does it have to do with me?"

"My point to this story is this," Maude went on. "Proceed as you've planned, but don't expect things to go smoothly or that the outcome will be as you expect or desire. That you have the courage to begin this undertaking is worthy of admiration. However, your quest is a dangerous one. Be careful! Don't talk to everyone about this. Some can't be trusted. As for your father, he'd be proud. You see, I grew up in Kotzebue like your father. Why do you need to know this story? Because the boy in the story was he.

"Talk to Sam Rawbones," said Maude. "Sam cared for your father's team when brought back to Nome after found at the river. He will help give you some understanding of the situation."

"I don't think Sam can make things better for me," said Kort.

"No," said Maude, "but he can add a little knowledge of what he saw, helping you to understand more."

"Yes, I see," said Kort. "Thanks for everything."

Maude fills his small pack with cookies, gives him a hug and tells him he's welcome anytime. "Give my best to your mother."

Kort takes his time getting to Sam's dog shelter that evening. The thought of Father struggling for courage even as a young boy is hard to imagine. "I know I'm the same way," he said to himself.

When he reaches the shelter, Sam and a rough-looking native are hassling over money owed for services rendered.

"I'm not paying for your lousy service. You ask too much," hollered the native, a mean-looking character with matted black hair, a whiskered face, and missing front teeth.

Kort thinks he's seen him somewhere before.

"Well, sorry you're not satisfied. I do my best. You can always make a trade if you don't have the money," Sam hollers back.

The native storms off nearly knocking Kort down on his way out.

"You forgot your dog harness. I mended it." The guy turns, grabs the harness circling it above his head as if to strike Sam.

"Looks like you lost a customer," said Kort, surprised at such behavior.

"Some people you can never satisfy but, Weyahok, he'll come back, he always does.

"Did you call him Weyahok?" asks Kort.

"Yeah," answered Sam. "Why?"

"Well… how's my team?" asked Kort, allowing Sam to cool down before asking any questions about Weyahok.

"Go check for yourself. Have I ever not taken care of your dogs?"

"Always," assures Kort as he walks off to see the team.

"I'll put my work away and go fix us a bite to eat," said Sam.

"What's on your mind, boy?" asks Sam, as they rest after a light meal of blubber broth and dried berries. "Something bothering you?"

Kort explains his search for the truth concerning his father's death. He doesn't reveal as much to Sam as he did to Maude. "I've heard plenty about Weyahok. He's not really trusted. Can you trust him?" asks Kort.

Sam shrugs his shoulders and then adds, "You need to mind your own business. You're only going to get hurt if you pursue this."

"I need to ask you a few more questions, please," said Kort. "You found my father's body in the river?" Kort asks. "What did you see when you got there?"

"Yes. John Kamik and Thomas Tomuk were with me."

"I don't remember that Thomas went," said Kort in a surprised tone.

"Yes, he said he was a close friend of your father's. Said he wanted to help."

"No. He wasn't a close friend," Kort expresses, shaking his head.

"Of course," Sam put in. "Everyone knew how your father felt about him. No one wanted to argue with him, so he went."

"Anyway," continues Sam, "Lucia was laying on the sled when we arrived. Once your father's body was raised from the river and put on the sled, Lucia was ready to leave." Sam choked up a little having said that and excuses himself for a minute.

When he returns, Kort thanks him for getting his father. "Was father wearing a gold nugget when pulled from the river?"

"No, he wasn't," Sam said. "I'd seen it before when the local shaman was here trying to sell his wares. Your father was here getting his team ready to head back to Candle. The gold nugget was on the outside of his clothing. Realizing it, he quickly placed it inside. But the shaman had spotted it and asked him to trade it for something of value he had. Your father told him it wasn't for sale or trade. It would belong to his son. The shaman said nothing and left. Your mother has the nugget, doesn't she?"

"No," said Kort.

"Well, then, it must be in the river," said Sam.

"I don't think so," said Kort. "It was attached by a thin piece of rawhide woven around sinew thread. Father couldn't' slip it over his head. He never took it off. The strap would have to be cut. Thomas Tomuk told me to look for it because it's 'closer than I think.'"

"That doesn't make sense," added Sam, frowning. "Well, so anyway, when we returned to Nome, I cared for the team. Lucia lay on some straw and moaned. Wouldn't eat. Figured she was hurting… and missing her master."

"Was she injured?" asked Kort.

"I'm sure I've told you this," said Sam. "She had a nasty welt across her nose and a large knot on her head. Probably harness burns. She was limping… most likely from exhaustion."

"No, Sam," Kort said loudly. "Father was an expert at fitting harnesses. His dogs never had harness burns. Someone struck her when she tried to help Father. We all know Thomas beats his dogs."

"Your father's death was an accident," Sam pleads.

"It wasn't an accident," yells Kort. "I'm sure of it and aim to prove it. The shaman you mentioned," continues Kort. "Did he sell amulets like this one?" taking it from his pocket.

"Yes, similar, but not with initials… not unless asked to have them put on."

"Wouldn't you say this one belongs to Konok Weyahok?" asks Kort.

As if guessing what Kort would say next, Sam beat him to it. "No, Weyahok didn't kill your father. He acts tough, but he's all talk. Besides your father taught him a lesson. He never approached him again. Isn't it stretching it a bit to connect an amulet with the death of your father?"

"I think the amulet was given to help me find the truth," admits Kort.

Sam just shook his head. "By the way," he said, "Your uncle stopped by today. Said the whale hunt begins late tomorrow morning. He'll meet you at the postal station. Just bring your gear."

That night Kort tosses and turns. Why did it seem everyone he talks to is protecting someone? Why don't they want him to find the truth? Why? He owes it to Father. He must be as bold as he was… this was proving to be true.

Next morning the post master hands him a small piece of folded paper. "This was on my desk this morning. Has your name on it."

Kort unfolds the paper. It reads: Stop making trouble for yourself. Go home where you belong.

"Are you coming?" yells Nuevat, Uncle Melvin's fishing partner. "We don't have all day."

Kort grabs his gear and hurries out the door. *Why do I fear this whaling adventure?* he thought as he heads to the wharf.

CHAPTER 11

GRAMPUSES ATTACK

A bitter wind penetrates the air as Kort hurries to the landing with gear pack slung over his shoulder.

When he arrives, Uncle Melvin is stocking his umiak with provisions for the trip. Nuevat sets the single blade paddles in place.

"Did you remember your seal bladder rain gear?" Uncle Melvin urges. "We can run into rough seas."

"Got them right here," Kort assures, holding them up. He remembers his father telling him the umiak is the strongest and largest of boats used by their people. It can carry thirty passengers and over a ton of cargo. Easy to maneuver and very fast, the umiak can propel them swiftly to their destination and back, providing the sea cooperates.

"Max Clayes, a Canadian friend and whaler will be coming with us," Melvin made known, glancing at Nuevat. "You all know I don't like too many whalers on my boat, but Max is an experienced man of the sea. Good to have him along."

Sadly, Kort thinks, Max will take Father's place. But the thought of throwing a harpoon put a smile on his face. Father would want that.

He was boyer the few times he'd been whaling. That's how a boy begins—as an errand boy. One who fetches things for the crew.

A ladder extends down to reach the umiak from the four-foot-thick ice bank above the ocean. Kort climbs down and settles in.

Narrow seats and the boat skeleton are made from driftwood logs. Waterproof walrus hide covers the boat exterior.

"Welcome aboard," Melvin greets as Max Clayes comes down the ladder.

Max is a tall, hefty guy with a small gray braid resting against the back of his neck. Thick gray eyebrows shade his dark eyes. A faded blue handkerchief tied around his forehead disappears as he quickly pulls his parka hood up over his head.

"Good to see you," Melvin says, smiling.

"Put 'er there," replies Max, extending his hand for a shake.

"Meet Kort Olanna, my nephew, and this is Nuevat Weyahok, my fishing buddy."

Nuevat glares at Max and then at Melvin. "Bad luck having a white guy on board. He'll only bring us trouble."

"Oh, don't pay attention to him," Melvin exclaims facing Nuevat. "He's our bad luck."

Max moves his head in agreement, pausing to give Nuevat a sober look.

Kort has never seen such a big man. He towers over Melvin and Nuevat. The size of his hands would triple one of his own.

Once they settle in, the umiak pulls out to sea… destination, the Bering Strait.

"In April," Melvin begins, "whales traveling northward come in closer to shore, which can make whaling a bit easier, right, Max?"

"You're right," Max agrees. "So, I understand, this whaling venture will stretch from Nome to Wales."

"Sure hope we have a successful hunt," Kort adds, trying to get into the conversation. He remembers a few years ago when no one in the village harpooned a whale. Many went hungry. The villagers chewed on seal blubber to satisfy growling stomachs.

"Stay clear of those ice blocks floating about," warns Melvin. Hitting one can cause problems."

Nuevat and Max are steering the umiak. Suddenly a wave strikes a large ice block plunging it into the sea.

"Keep your eyes focused out there, boys, and watch for whales too!" Melvin said, gently reminding them.

"So, Nuevat," Kort inquires, "did my uncle say your last name is Weyahok?"

"Yeah, you heard right," Nuevat answers.

"So did your cousin, Konok, make this amulet?" Kort asks, hoping for information from him.

"What's it to you anyway?" Nuevat said angrily.

"Kort, be quiet. This is a whale hunt," Melvin orders. "Don't disturb him."

"Just want to ask if this amulet was made by his cousin," Kort admits, with some hesitation.

"Let me see that," said Max, taking it with one free hand off the boat oar. "Why do you have this? You're a Christian, aren't you?" Max frowns.

"Howard Yekut gave it to me before I left for Nome. Said it would give protection, but I only took it to find out who it belongs to."

Handing it to Nuevat, Max shook his head. "So, is this your cousin's amulet?"

"Yeah, it's his," Nuevat said, rolling it over in his hand. So what?"

"Do you see Konok often?" Kort presses on.

"Knock it off, Kort. We've heard enough. Watch for whales," Melvin orders.

"So, Father Le Roux's your pastor?" Max asks Kort, placing both hands back on the oar. "He comes from Dawson City in the Northern Territory. Same as me. We grew up together. Know his family real well."

"Just can't imagine Father Le Roux as a little boy," Kort admits.

"Yeah," continues Max, "he was the fastest runner in the neighborhood."

"Met your father when he and Bronze Browning delivered mail in Dawson years ago. Good man, your father."

"Yes, for sure. He was the best," boasts Kort.

"Yeah, he came upon bad luck a few times, though, didn't he?" Nuevat sneers, glaring at Kort.

That guy is bad company, Kort thought, continuing to glance out to sea.

Waves build up as they approach Kings Island, where they'll spend the night. They pull the umiak ashore. After chowing down on fresh seal provided by Melvin, they bed in the umiak for the night.

"Have a good night," Melvin mumbles with a yawn. "We'll head out early morning."

King's Island is a haven for walruses. Their loud lowing resembles the mooing of a herd of cattle. They keep their distance from the umiak, but it is easy to figure out trespassers aren't welcome. The huge males guard the herd, annoying Kort with infernal sounds. Sleep doesn't come easily.

"Come on, you guys," Melvin hollers, shaking Kort's shoulder. "Morning is here and there's a whale out there waiting for us."

A large tin of hot broth is steaming over a fire on the sand as the crew pulls on their kamiks.

"Drink down and we'll be out to sea," Melvin urges rolling the hide covers up.

Placing the umiak back in the water after Nuevat douses the fire, they board the boat.

"Better watch those icebergs to the north, Nuevat. We're getting too close," Max stresses.

"Those icebergs crashing down are proof there's a battle between the spirit powers and the sea," Nuevat said with certainty. "It's dangerous for us to be around them."

"Oh, you can't possibly believe that," scoffs Max. "That's an ancient belief of your native people."

"Yeah," put in Kort, "don't you believe in creation?"

"I think both of you are crazy," Nuevat grumbles. "I only need the shaman."

"Pay attention to the sea," hollers Melvin.

"Look to the west. Killer whales after a bowhead."

"Max and Nuevat lift their oars to watch the killer whales.

Kort's attention focuses on a fountain of spray rising from the sea. "Wow, that's a huge bowhead!" he bursts out. "There must be four or five killer whales after it."

"Grampuses!" Max declares. "They must be ten or twelve feet long. The most dangerous thing in the ocean."

"Watch," orders Nuevat. "It'll be real gruesome."

Kort remembers his father saying that grampuses or killer whales are the gluttons of the sea, eating more than their own weight at one meal.

"Oh, they're awful critters, aren't they?" Kort groans, watching the killers exhaust the bowhead. "Why, are we watching this?"

"Well, grampuses have their purpose—like everything," assures Melvin. "They're also known as orcas or blackfish—a toothed, flesh-eating whale related to the dolphin."

"I didn't know that," Kort admits.

The big whale keeps diving into the sea, but he dives too quickly before getting enough air and comes up sooner than he would have. The killer whales rush at him from every angle. They spring into the air, smash into his head, and dash into his eyes. He can't escape. Battered, blinded, fatigued and dazed, he drops his jaw at last.

"Just what the grampuses are waiting for," Melvin declares. "Now they'll start tearing out large chunks of tongue. That's a delicate morsel to them—it weighs almost a ton."

Kort has never seen such a spectacle. "What do we do now, Uncle Melvin?" he asks, thinking they might take this whale as soon as the killers leave.

"Just wait 'til they go. They'll be back for their prize, so we won't spend time dragging it off. We'll fetch some baleen, though, for shoeing sleds. Besides the victors have a right to their trophy."

They make their way cautiously to the big whale, watching for the grampuses' return. The whole surface of the sea surrounding the whale is stained dark with blood. Like an island he floats, rolling with the wash of the waves.

They steer close to its head.

"The open mouth is like a great cave," Kort cites. "Ten men could easily fit inside."

"The jagged black bone hanging from the middle of the jaw is baleen or whalebone," put in Max.

"Some of the huge ones must be six or seven feet long," Nuevat adds.

"These parts are used to strain everything that comes into his mouth," Melvin instructs. "Only small creatures go down its throat, which is the size of my fist." He demonstrates, clenching his hand.

With the ivory butt of his harpoon, Melvin breaks off several pieces of baleen. Kort places them in the bottom of the umiak.

"There, we have all we need," said Melvin.

"Let's get out of here, then," Nuevat insists nervously, "before the killers return."

So, they travel northward for bowhead whales.

"Speed is necessary," Nuevat mutters. "We're traveling too slow."

"You're wrong," protests Max. "It takes patience. You should know that."

"Yeah," agrees Kort. "Patience, not speed."

"You know nothing about this, so keep quiet," Nuevat roars, raising his hand to strike Kort.

"Mustn't do that," Max quickly speaks out, blocking Nuevat's arm.

"How could a mama's boy know anything about patience?" accuses Nuevat. "You've never had to deal with anything difficult in your life. Of course, suppose you suffered some, not getting the gold nugget promised…."

Silence follows as Melvin and Nuevat stare at each other.

"Storm's approaching," Melvin declares, noticing the heavy clouds sagging down to the surface of the sea.

White spray drifts along the horizon to the south, like steam across water, where waves are lashed to a froth by the wind. White caps race past and the wind sings overhead.

"Hey, guys," Max urges, "better start shoveling out water from the bottom of the boat."

In the process, Nuevat trips, falling overboard.

"Grab him quick or he'll drown," shouts Melvin. "Can't swim."

Max and Kort grab his swinging arms pulling him back in the boat.

"Here," offers Kort, handing Max his bear hide to wrap him in.

"I see land to the east," Melvin declares. "Shoreline of Wales. Safer to stay there; let the storm pass and return to sea in the morning."

CHAPTER 12

DOUBLE CAPTURE

When on shore, Nuevat sits by the fire Max built to dry out. It takes some time for him to quit shaking. The crackling blaze feels comforting to all of them sitting nearby sipping on bone broth.

"Let's get our forty winks so we can handle the adventure tomorrow," Melvin remarks. "I've had enough for today."

Morning brings a peaceful outlook. Nuevat still shivers a little, but he helps prepare the harpoons and seal bladder floats. The floats are used to slow down and tire a whale once harpooned.

"Everyone on board," Melvin chuckles. "Our whale is waiting."

"Today will be a better day," Max said, looking for a guarantee from Nuevat as they head out.

Nuevat unrolls the seal bladder floats. A wounded whale can run for days. It is a true test of endurance for an umiak crew to keep up.

They no more oar out for the hunt when Melvin hollers, "West!" pointing his arm in that direction. "Bowhead whales! Maybe three of them."

The whales are traveling north slowly. As the umiak gets closer, Kort can see a large whale and a couple smaller one.

"Must be a family," he reckons, grabbing his harpoon.

Steering the umiak up and around the whales drive them closer to the shoreline. The whales aren't in a hurry. They dive, surface, blow water from their lungs, and dive again. The younger ones appear to play carelessly. Now and then leaping into the air like porpoises trying to stand on their heads. The threshing of their tails sound like the roar of several waterfalls. They seem forgetful of their approaching doom.

"Grab your harpoons!" hollers Melvin. "This is as close as we'll get. You throw first, Kort."

Kort threw with all his might. "Yah-hoo," he yells, hitting the medium size whale smack-dab in the head. Max threw his and hit below the mouth. Melvin and Nuevat miss. They pull their harpoons back using the attached ropes. They propel them again, this time penetrating its side.

The harpooned whale continues to move ahead with the umiak in pursuit. The crew paddles as they've never paddled before.

"You okay, Kort?" Max asks, noticing him rubbing his arms and appearing somewhat dazed.

"Yeah, I'm okay. Just determined this whale's not getting away."

"For sure," Melvin agrees. "You're a whale hunter now. Your harpoon struck it first."

Max heaves the seal bladder float up over its head.

Hours pass. The whale is slowing and its dives into the ocean are less frequent. Once again, the umiak comes closer.

"Throw your harpoon again." Melvin signals to Kort. "One more time should do it."

He thrusts the harpoon just as the whale turns toward them, hitting it below the eye.

With what seems its last scrap of energy, it dives, heading straight for the umiak and leaving a trail of blood in its wake.

"Down on the deck," orders Melvin. "We're in for a jolting ride."

A jolting ride it is! No words can express the umiak's battle with the restless, irresistible waves caused by the struggling whale. At times, Kort thinks, they are bound to capsize, for the bowhead is under the boat trying to do just that.

Finally, it surfaces, giving them a shower blowing water from its lungs. It makes one last sharp turn smashing its tail against the umiak. Finally, it tumbles, wallows and, from sheer exhaustion, floats on the sea.

"It's given up!" shouts Kort, wanting to jump in the air. "Boy, I'm glad it's over but so happy to be a whale hunter now."

"You did a great job," Max declares. "Your father would be so proud."

"Thanks to all of you for letting me strike first," Kort said, grinning. "I know any of you could've taken that whale."

"Don't thank me," Nuevat insults, looking at Melvin. "I was told not to strike first. If I had, I'd sell the whale and make a profit for myself."

"Oh, no, you wouldn't," Melvin snaps, "'cause you'd owe the crew some whale."

"I'd work my way around that," Nuevat sneers.

"You'd find yourself in trouble with the law as well," assures Max.

Nuevat quiets down.

They sit back on the umiak seats taking in deep breaths and surveying their prize. Securing the huge catch with ropes, they hasten to the shoreline of King's Island to ready their vessel and whale for the voyage home.

On shore, Melvin builds a fire, heats bone broth and fetches some dried ptarmigan from a pack.

"We'll need to take turns as guards until morning," Melvin decides. "Grampuses or thieves might deprive us of our catch."

"You're first up, young whaler," Melvin said, looking quite serious. "I'll take the next watch after I have a few hours' sleep."

"Okay," agrees Kort. "I'll eat first, though. I'm really hungry."

"Well," adds Max, "first-time whalers usually don't eat at all. That's part of becoming a genuine whale hunter. You want to be tough, don't you?"

"Sure, but I struck first so I should get to eat, right?" Kort blurts out, raising both arms.

"You're just a whiner," complains Nuevat.

"You'll get something to eat," said Melvin. Now go to the shore and take your rifle."

Kort sits on a rock near the secured whale with rifle in one hand. Listening to his growling stomach doesn't make sitting on watch any easier. *Those guys sure like to pick on me*, he thought. Getting back to Candle with whale meat and blubber will be great. Mother and Nimette will be proud of me.

The rhythm of lapping waves hitting the frosty shoreline causes Kort to doze every so often. Suddenly men's voices coming from the sea arouse him. He stands from his perch with rifle in hand.

A boat with three men pull ashore. Darkness prevents getting a good look, but by the sound of their voices they aren't native, maybe European. Kort backs up closer to the fire.

The older guy pulls a revolver from his parka aiming it at Kort.

"You've got our whale. We've been following you. You'll come with us to face the law. Hand over the rifle."

Just then Max appears behind Kort, grabs the rifle and shoots the older one in the shoulder. He falls to the ground rolling and groaning.

Kort completely stunned by this experience, having never seen someone shot, moves from side to side seeking escape.

Melvin quickly crawls in, grabs the guy's revolver from the ground and holds it on the other two.

"What's going on here?" hollers Nuevat rubbing his eyes as he comes close to the fire.

"Some trouble," said Melvin. "We need your help. Quick! Get a dressing for this guy's wound."

"Kort! Don't just stand there. Help Nuevat put a dressing on his shoulder," Max orders. "I'll get the rope and we'll tie these guys up."

Kort is so dazed he has difficulty helping. "I've never seen someone…," he begins, but stops when Nuevat shakes him.

"There's a first time for everything."

Once the bad guys are tied up, Max gives Nuevat an order. "You get to haul these guys to the authorities in Nome. Turn their revolver in as well. If you head out now, you'll get there before we do. Just travel the shoreline."

"Why me?" complains Nuevat. "You take them."

"I need to stay with Melvin and Kort to get the whale to Nome," Max remarks.

"Once their umiak is loaded with the three guys and Nuevat, Max stands by their boat.

"Make sure you get them to Nome," Max sternly orders, staring at Nuevat. "We'll be behind you and see you there."

Kort and Melvin prepare their umiak for departure. Bone broth is sizzling on the fire as they wait for Max to come up from the shore.

"Guess we can take off too," Max pants as he steps close to the fire. "We shouldn't be too far behind them."

"Yeah," agrees Melvin. "You think you should tell Kort who you are?"

"What do you mean?" Kort asks. "You're not Max Clayes?"

"Oh, yeah, for sure I'm Max Clayes… a Mountie."

"You mean you're a Royal Canadian Mountie?" Kort stutters in disbelief. "Boy," Kort confesses, "I've never met a Mountie before."

"Well, now you have," put in Melvin.

"Yes," Max laughs, "and I really don't like water but your good Black Robe insisted I go along on this hunt to keep an eye on you."

"Uncle Melvin, I can't believe you'd let someone on the umiak who doesn't like water."

"I had to," Melvin said. "Mounties have more importance than me."

"But to add a more serious tone to all of this," Max adds, "we must be watchful of the goings-on around us, starting now."

CHAPTER 13

A PRICE TO PAY

The journey back to Nome with their captured whale attached by ropes to the umiak, gives Kort time to sift through his thoughts.

It seems as though everyone knows more of what's going on than me. Max is on this hunt to watch out for me? The thieves were going to take me with them. Why? Now Max says we must be watchful of everything around us. One thing I'm certain of, Father Le Roux believes what I've told him.

The sound of the community bell alerts the natives that a whale catch is coming to shore. They crowd the surrounding area to get a glimpse.

"Looks like we'll have plenty of help hoisting this whale to the landing," said Melvin.

"Yeah, for sure," agrees Max, "but I don't see the umiak with Nuevat and the tough guys."

"Where do you suppose they are?" fears Kort.

"We might find out soon," Max predicts. "I see a couple Mounties on shore."

Several natives held ropes to lift the whale from the ice bank.

"Thanks for your help!" Melvin hollers, climbing the ladder to shake their hands.

"You need help!" one native insists. "Small crews can't handle this much meat."

"Well, we started out with four," Max put in, but… say, did a boat pull in before us with four guys… one wounded?"

"No," chimes in several guys. "You're the first boat this morning."

"Wonder what happened to them?" Kort burst out as Melvin and Max look at each other.

"We'll help you slice up this critter," offer the natives, drawing their knives.

"Thanks!" said Melvin. "Kort, fetch the meat sacks."

"I'll go chat with those Mounties for a while, then be back to help," said Max. "See if they have some news. You stay with your uncle, Kort."

By the time Max returns, Kort has filled four meat sacks.

"There's still more meat and plenty of blubber to pack," Kort tells Max.

"We'll have lots to share with the community, right, Uncle Melvin?" Kort boasts.

"That's for sure. And all these good helpers as well," adds Melvin.

"Well, my, my! Just look what my boy caught!"

"Mother!" Kort jumps up to give her a big hug. "And Nimette! I didn't expect to see you here."

"You don't think we'd miss your first whale catch, do you?" asks Mother.

"And what about me?" said Father Le Roux, walking from behind a group of natives.

"This is just great," Kort said, wearing a wide grin. "What a surprise!"

"Come on," Melvin urges. "Let's get this whale cut up and bagged. Then we can take care of other things."

Max and a few more natives help. Even Father Le Roux rolled up his sleeves. Mother and Nimette rounded up a few more seal-skin bags.

Several hours pass before they finish. All who helped took their share. The rest was divided between Melvin, Max, and Kort.

"What about Nuevat's share?" asks Kort.

"Oh, he won't be needing it for a while," Max answers. "Besides you'll be taking most of it back to Candle to share with the community."

"The Nome community has a celebration planned tomorrow for this young whale hunter," announces Mother. "Maude Blaufuss is helping with that."

"You'll be worn out from festivities," adds Melvin, "once the Candle community has theirs."

"Unfortunately, all this happy conversation must end for now," Max sighs. "We have some business to take care of."

"With all this help let's get these whale bags in the ice block storage," said Melvin.

"We need to head over to the postal station. The elders are holding a private meeting there," said Max.

"I need to check on my team," said Kort, anxiously.

"I'll go for you," offers Nimette.

"Yes," agrees Mother, good idea. Kort needs to be at this meeting. He's earned it."

"What's all this about?" Kort begs.

"You'll soon find out," promises Melvin. "But remember, once this meeting begins, that you remain quiet. Ask no questions."

Entering the postal station, Kort is directed to a back room used for storing mailbags and supplies for mail sleds. All he can see in the room are people. His eyes immediately catch sight of three Candle elders; Howard Yekut, Old Bill Keok, and Thomas Tomuk. But Thomas, seated between Howard and Old Bill, has his hands tied together. Bronze Browning and Maude Blaufuss are there as well.

Kort wants to speak, but he glances at Mother who has her finger to her lips.

Old Bill Keok, elder in-charge, stands to address the people with his eyes settling on Kort.

"The elders of Candle had their suspicions about the so-called accidental death of Brower Olanna, your father. We knew he was pretty incapable of foolhardy mistakes when it came to driving the mail sled. But we argued it could be possible he made a mistake and drowned in the river. We were also aware he had some enemies… those he'd corrected at times or tried to teach a lesson to. Yes, it was possible someone had harmed him. But it wasn't until you were so interested on knowing about Weyahok, that it made us stop to think."

Old Bill was tired and asked Howard to continue for a bit.

"So, giving you the amulet with the initials on it," begins Howard, "was in hopes you'd continue your pursuit with all of us watching out for you. The local shaman here in Nome had made the amulet and gave it to Konok who put his initials K.W. on it. Konok believed, as many natives do, in the potency of the amulet. So, the shaman became involved in all of this as you'll find out." Then Old Bill takes over again and Howard sits beside Thomas.

"As elders of the Candle community," Old Bill says, "it is our duty to uphold law and order in our village. Therefore, Thomas Tomuk has wronged the Olanna family and he must give his public confession to them before he is sentenced."

It is so quiet in the large room you could've heard a pin drop. Thomas stands and comes forward. He takes a few deep breaths, scans the room, resting his eyes on Kort. Then lowers them to the floor.

"Brower Olanna was good… too good," he begins. "Everyone always said that… even the shaman. He had the habit of always correcting someone who'd wronged him or been unjust to others. Oh, he wasn't perfect, for sure. Just irritated me so much I wished him… wished him… hurt."

Kort doesn't want to listen to him… wants to leave but knows he can't. He glances at Mother, who is totally at peace, which strengthens him.

Thomas continues, "All the gods seemed to smile on him and… it irritated me." He is briefly silent and begins to weep. "I never wanted him dead… I just wanted what he had. His dogs were the best… his patience the best… everything was. I hated him… and yet… and yet… I wanted to be just like him." He pauses to wipe his nose and clear his throat.

"Listen, Kort," he said, tears falling from his eyes. "I took your pup 'cause… 'cause you wouldn't let me have him. I put it in the icy stream to let it die there. No matter how hard I tried to win your favor, it never worked. Like being grateful for your father teaching me to whale hunt or telling you the gold nugget was closer than you think… nothing ever worked. Always wanted a son like you… never had one."

It is difficult for Kort to have compassion for Thomas because of the pain he's caused the family. Can he ever forgive him?

"Nuevat," Thomas sighs, "took the medal belonging to your mother and worn by your father when they… they… and Konok took the gold nugget. Nuevat gave me the medal to keep me quiet. I never would have gotten involved if I'd known what they were going to do with him. Believe me," he wept, "I didn't want him dead. I did wrong… but… I never wanted him dead."

Kort, shaking his head in disbelief, can't relate to what he's hearing and, yet, he'd suspected Thomas all along.

The emotional Thomas is moved back to his place and Old Bill returns.

"The local shaman here in Nome," Old Bill said, "made the amulet and gave it to Konok. Konok put his initials on it believing in its potency. The shaman happened to be passing the river when Konok and Nuevat were doing their dreadful deed. So, the shaman told them he'd help by driving Brower's dog team away. The team hadn't gone into the river, yet Lucia was the only one injured. But when the shaman came near her, she jumped at him causing a tear in his neck. He had a severe cut and needed to have it tended to in Nome. Said he'd tell the authorities how it happened."

"That's when Nuevat," Old Bill continues, "gave him the gold nugget telling him to keep quiet and they'd sell it and share the proceeds. But the shaman never let go of it, always threatening that he'd tell who killed Brower Olanna. They apparently were afraid to do away with the shaman for they feared his spiritual powers," finishes Old Bill.

"So, to conclude with our part," Old Bill adds, and as elders of Candle representing the law of this community, we therefore sentence Thomas Tomuk, as a penalty, to help provide for the Olanna family for as long as necessary but no less than five years."

Old Bill takes a long, hard look at Kort. Kort doesn't want Thomas to help his family and Old Bill probably figures that, for the frown on his face is sure to be revealing.

Before taking his seat, Old Bill concludes, "Mountie Max asks permission to speak and then Father Le Roux."

"It's necessary to give you the information I have on Nuevat and the thieves he was to deliver to Nome," Max begins.

Melvin is shifting back and forth in his standing position. Nuevat is his friend.

"When Nuevat was given orders to take the thieves to Nome," begins Max, "he instead headed north and freed them on a shore past Wales. You see, Kort, they were given orders to capture you and throw you overboard. Why? Because you were getting too close to the truth about your father. They were friends of Konok's and hired to do you harm. In fact, they were the culprits your father stopped from holding the native's head in the water trough several years ago. Luckily, the Mounties caught up with all three of them in Wales. Konok was taken this morning in Nome.

Konok and Nuevat were jealous of your father. They wanted the gold nugget. The nugget, they believed would give them power and the admiration of the community. For many natives, nothing disturbs the mind more than to assume they stand alone against the crowd. They'd convinced themselves that Brower was admired and honored because of the gold nugget. Nuevat, Konok and the thieves will be taken to Mountie headquarters in Dawson City."

Kort is fighting back tears as Father Le Roux comes forward to speak. Letting his eyes center on the Olanna family, he said, "Kort, we are all here to let you know you were right. Your father's death wasn't an accident. Your firm belief in his steadfast ways and reliable service have passed the test. You've secured and saved his honor. We all commend you for your dedication to this cause bringing it all to the surface. And, I might add, your father would be so proud."

CHAPTER 14

FORGIVENESS BRINGS PEACE

Martha and Nimette stay with Maude Blaufuss that evening and help with food preparation for the celebration the next day.

"My goodness," said Maude, "there's lots to do."

"For sure," Martha agrees. "Inuit women will spend a whole night preparing for one of these festivities. I've done it many times."

"I'm tired just thinking about it," Maude admits. "But let's get to it. Several other women are preparing food as well."

"Yes, of course," Martha said, "as she slices mikigaq, a fermented whale meat black in color and much loved by the natives.

"I'm not real fond of mikigaq myself," Maude adds, "but I know that natives view it as a delicacy."

"The Candle elders will surely boil the whales entrails over an open fire. It's an Inuit favorite," said Martha.

"Well, this old German gal will skip that," Maude laughs. "Oh, my," Maude recalls, "and a couple women are bringing caribou fat they will melt over the fire. Once it's cooled, the young girls... you Nimette... can make akutuq—Eskimo ice cream."

"I'm so excited to do that. It's so much fun!"

"Never made it myself," said Maude, "but I've tasted it. Explain how it's made."

"Well," begins Nimette, "Mother says it's a recipe passed down from generation to generation. The caribou fat, once melted over an open fire, must be cooled in a large container. Using your hands, tossing it over and over to whip air into it until it thickens. You place it on an ice block to keep it cold. Then add berries. So good!"

The next day Kort harnesses his team to the sled to help bring the food to the hall. Father Le Roux is in front of the hall when he brings the last load.

"There's plenty of young guys here to haul this inside," said Father Le Roux to Kort.

He stands outside with the Black Robe before the celebration begins.

"So when did you start believing me?" Kort asks.

"Oh, I guess it was when I corrected you for pointing fingers at others and you told me 'shouldn't I follow my heart?' I thought deeply about what you said, decided to get in touch with Max, and he began to do a little investigating."

"So it all seems to fit together," Kort said somewhat annoyed. "It's over, but I don't want Thomas—"

"Things don't always turn out the way we'd like," Father Le Roux put in quickly. "Think about Thomas. This is about him. Remember the lesson your father had to learn… and accept. Having humility will help you to forgive your enemies. Forgiveness is the first step."

People begin to stream into the hall. It is exciting to see all those dressed in their native costumes. Several young men bring their seal-skin-covered drums. There'll be plenty of music, song, and dance. Kort thinks back when he was young and with his father at a whale celebration. Father was always asked to tell one of his personal stories and everyone settled down to listen. One in particular came to Kort's mind. His father was a young boy. Tuberculosis had spread through the community. Natives were dying and hunting was nearly at a complete stop. Food was scarce. His father's family had gone without food, except for stale blubber scraps, for many, many days. But one cold winter morning, Kort remembers his father saying, he found a breathing hole in the ice and caught a Ringed Neck Seal. Taking it back to the village, the family shared the one seal with the rest of the community reserving only a meager meal for themselves. Kort recalls his father saying, "It's better to give than to receive."

Thinking of today's celebration, surely Old Bill will tell some of his wild hard-to-believe stories. He'll get some good laughs. Many of the youngsters will recite poetry of the land, sea, and whales. Excitement fills Kort's mind.

It's great to see the turnout, he thought. The Nome elders, and of course, the Candle elders stand inside waiting for it to begin.

Thomas comes in with Old Bill Keok. His hands aren't tied any more. Thomas and Kort catch sight of each other about the same time.

It quiets down once Old Bill gives a short talk on the whale capture by Kort and whose son he is. Then the drums begin to beat and natives, young and old, in bright, colorful costumes dance.

Mother, Kort, and Nimette stand side by side swaying their feet back and forth to the rhythm of the drums.

Maude Blaufuss tells a story of her husband's first whale hunt adventure that everyone enjoys. Young ones recite poems of whale hunts and people lost at sea.

Finally, the food is laid out. They all share in the delicacies.

The late evening brings to a close this wonderful day.

Kort stands by Mother. They both seem to take a deep breath.

Looking at Kort she expresses, "Be a good example, Son. I want you to think of something you can do for Thomas."

He can't look at her right then for he is thinking he can hear his father saying the same thing.

Suddenly Old Bill speaks up loudly, "Kort, please come up front."

He is motionless for a moment wondering what all this means, then walks forward.

"Brower Olanna, an esteemed elder of Candle, acquired the title of Headsman for his constant bravery and pursuit of truth in the community. This is an honor given to those men worthy of it. Now," Old Bill continues, "his son, Kort, not an adult but certainly deserving, the elders agree to make an exception by offering him the title of Honorary Junior Headsman for his non-stop hunt for truth and unmatched bravery in difficult circumstances."

The "yeahs" and clapping from all inside is deafening. Kort is overwhelmed.

When the excitement dies down, Old Bill concludes, "Kort, your duty now is to be a good example to the youth. Always to help where you are needed."

"Thank you," Kort gratefully answers. "I'll always try to be dependable."

Mother and Nimette hurry forward to hug him. "We're so proud of you, dear son… and brother," adds Nimette.

"Should we head home?" Mother asks, looking at Kort.

"Not quite yet," Kort said. "I've something to do." Thomas was standing by the door opening as Kort came to him.

"Thomas," Kort said determined to be pleasant. "Thanks for the apology. I'll work real hard to forgive you. It's something I must do… I want to do." As he starts to walk away, he turns again to Thomas, adding, "Oh, by the way, stop by our place this week, will you? I have a pup for you."

The look on Thomas' face is one of utter disbelief as he takes a few steps toward Kort.

"Thank you so much. You can be sure I'll take good care of him" The smile on Thomas's face said everything to Kort.

As Kort walks out of the hall, Father Le Roux gives him a pat on the shoulder. "Well done, young man. Your father would be proud."

He smiles at the Black Robe and walks to his team and sled. "Thanks, my dear father, peace has finally come back to me," he said aloud. "My anger's lifted."

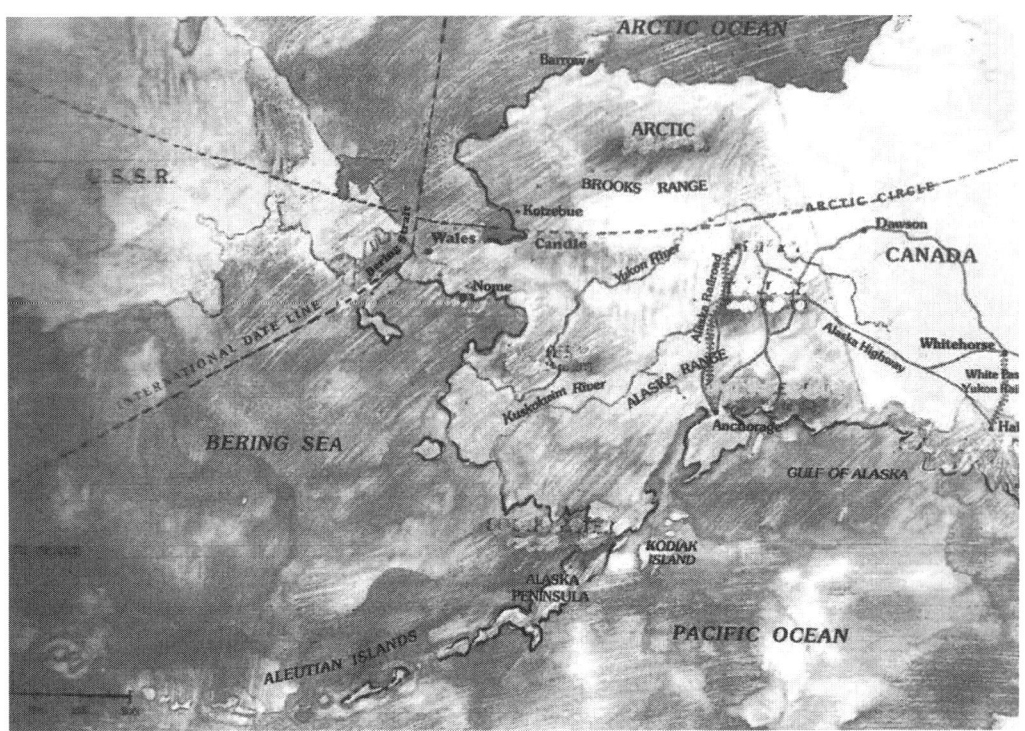

THE ALEUTS CALLED IT ALASHKA, or "The Great Land."

umiak

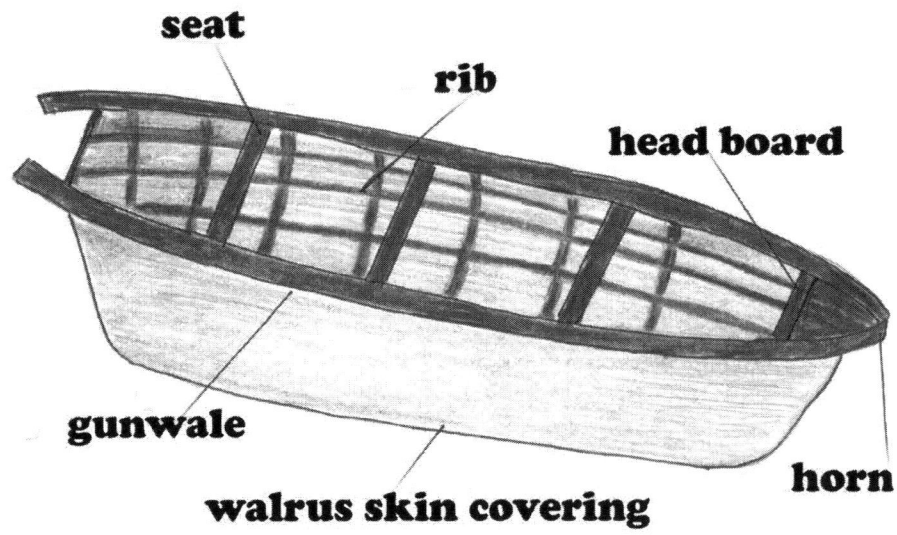

seat

rib

head board

gunwale

walrus skin covering

horn

Bear-Grease Cookies

- ❖ 2 eggs
- ❖ 3/4 cup milk
- ❖ 2/3 cup bear lard (rendered)
- ❖ 3/4 tsp. baking powder
- ❖ 1½ cups sugar or honey
- ❖ 3 cups flour, sifted
- ❖ ½ tsp. salt, 1 tsp. flavoring

Beat eggs and sugar, milk and bear lard. Beat until light and fluffy. Add flavoring. Then add sifted flour, salt and baking powder. (add more flour if needed) Roll-dough, cut out, bake on ungreased cookie sheet in quick, hot oven.